RECE

JUL 0

MADRONA

ANOTHER KIND OF HURRICANE

TAMARA ELLIS SMITH

schwartz & wade books · new york

In connection with the publication of this book, the author has made a donation to the nonprofit organization lowernine.org.

Visit us on the Web! randomhousekids.com

Educators and librarians, for a variety of teaching tools, visit us at RHTeachersLibrarians.com

Library of Congress Cataloging-in-Publication Data
Smith, Tamara Ellis.
Another kind of hurricane / Tamara Ellis Smith. — First edition.
    pages cm
Summary: The world itself seems to bring together Henry, whose best friend died near their home in the mountains of Vermont, and Zavion, who lost his home in Hurricane Katrina, so that the boys can help each other heal.
ISBN 978-0-553-51193-2 (hc) — ISBN 978-0-553-51194-9 (glb)
ISBN 978-0-553-51195-6 (ebook)
[1. Loss (Psychology)—Fiction. 2. Friendship—Fiction. 3. Death—Fiction. 4. Grief—Fiction. 5. Survival—Fiction. 6. Hurricane Katrina, 2005—Fiction.] I. Title.
PZ7.1.S657Ano 2015
[Fic]—dc23
2014030847

The text of this book is set in Belen.

Book design by Rachael Cole

Printed in the United States of America

2 4 6 8 10 9 7 5 3 1

First Edition

For everyone in New Orleans and Vermont whose lives were affected by Hurricane Katrina or Tropical Storm Irene— and for everyone who came to help.

And in memory of my grandmother Eleanor Ellis, a secret writer and real adventurer. If she were alive today, I know she'd take me on a garage-sale hunt for magic marbles.

From high in the sky, above the pathways of parrots, above cloud lines, above the blue—where the moon and the sun take turns shining over rivers and valleys, oceans and forests, towns and cities and farmland—from here you can see things.

To the south, a thick white wind chases its tail. Rain crashes down like an endless bucket of marbles tipped on its side. Fish dive deep to escape the deafening sound, stray dogs slink to the edges of buildings and press their bodies against the walls, people fill plastic bottles with water, push furniture against doors, grab the hands of their children and pull them up flights of stairs.

It is a hurricane.

From high in the sky, you can see the spiral of ocean water, moist air, and wind—and a boy in the middle of it all.

But that's not all you can see.

If you turn your head, if you look north, you can see another spiral. A spiral of sharp, cold air; a mountain; and another boy. Listen to the beating of his heart. Pounding, pelting, whoosh-ing like rain and wind. Inside the boy, rain falls like an endless bucket of marbles tipped on its side, and wind blows hard.

It is another kind of hurricane.

chapter 1
ZAVION

The wind wrapped itself around the two-by-fours that held Zavion's house straight and tall. The wind pushed and moaned just beneath the drywall. Papa had said they needed to get to the attic, to the highest point in the house.

But the attic didn't seem high enough.

The wind snuck through the walls. First blowing up and then pounding. Then sideways. Pound. Then down. Pound. Then down again with a piercing squeal. Zavion didn't know where he would feel it, or where he would hear it next. His teeth chattered. He squeezed his eyes shut, but that didn't stop the wind and that didn't stop his body from shaking so hard he thought his heart might shake right out of his chest.

Zavion closed his eyes and pictured Grandmother Mountain. He imagined climbing to its top. A real mountain would rise above this wind and Zavion would be safe.

* * *

"Zavion!" Papa called through the wind. He sounded far away, but he was only downstairs.

"Papa!"

"I'm coming up!"

Zavion's eyes darted around the room. Nothing was where it should be. Papa's rolls of canvas caught and tore on nails protruding from the walls. They flapped in the wind like shredded flags. Zavion crawled over to the window and held on to the sill. He peeked outside. It was morning, but it seemed as if the wind had blown the hours forward into night.

The dark sky poured rain on Zavion's street. Only it wasn't a street anymore. It was a river. The wind came again and Zavion's hands shook as he gripped the wooden sill. He pressed his chin against his hands to still them, but then his chin shook too.

Outside lay an enormous oak tree split in half. A work boot, jammed between two dangling branches. A lamp, sucked in and out of the water. A piece of the roof had broken off his neighbors' house and sped down the river. Someone clung to the roof. He strained his eyes to see who it was and— Was it? Yes. His neighbor's daughter. Zavion took care of her sometimes. It was so easy to make her laugh.

The wind gusted. She slipped on the wet roof.

Zavion closed his eyes. When he opened them again, a man was pulling the little girl out of the water.

The attic was definitely not high enough. It was not the top of a mountain. A mountain would rise above this.

This was the end of the world.

Zavion had lost all control—for only the second time ever—and this was the end of the world.

Zavion's fingers dug into the wood on the sill. He tried to calm himself. He remembered the bench outside his school where he sat to tie his sneakers before he ran home every afternoon after cross-country practice. His bed neatly made with his pillow squared and his book tucked into the top right corner. His peanut butter and honey sandwiches wrapped in wax paper and lined up in the refrigerator.

"Sweet Jesus!" Papa stood, soaking wet, at the top of the attic stairs. "The first floor. It's flooded. Sweet Jesus. I couldn't save anything."

"What about your paintings?" asked Zavion.

"All my murals. All my paintings. They're gone." Papa dropped an armful of cereal boxes and two cartons of juice onto the floor. "This was all I could get."

"What about the second floor?"

"I don't know. Everything is shaking—"

"What about my room? Mama's mural?"

"Oh, Zavion, I just don't know—"

"I'll get the survival kit," said Zavion. He'd made it himself, put it in the downstairs hall closet. He'd check on his mural when he went to get it.

"There are water moccasins down there, Zav. Snakes swimming in our kitchen."

"What?"

"You're not going downstairs." Papa stood like a fence in front of the stairway, but his eyes moved frantically around the room. "We have to leave."

Zavion pulled ruined canvases over to the window, and he and Papa waved them like flags, trying to get the attention of the helicopter flying overhead. But it kept on going.

The wind gusted and flung Zavion to the attic floor.

"The walls are breaking," Papa said. "We have to get out of here."

The wind found a path that it liked. It was a violin bow then, squealing back and forth across the two-by-fours. Back and forth, back and forth. Screaming. It splintered the walls of the attic and set itself free. But the wind stayed inside Zavion. The screaming wind filled him. Stayed twisted around the bones in his body.

Zavion pulled himself up. He and Papa waved the white flags again, and this time, when a helicopter flew overhead, it shone its lights on them. But then it just kept on going.

It kept on going.

chapter 2

HENRY

Henry's legs ached to run, his breath and heart pounded in his ears. To run on the mountain, behind Wayne's house, in their small town in northern Vermont, half a continent away from the hurricane in Louisiana. Henry wanted to run on the mountain with Brae at his heels and Wayne by his side. Like the very last time.

"Brae's the starting line," said Henry, pointing to the large black and white dog sitting at his feet. "I taught him how to lie completely straight. Watch." Henry raised his arm. Then he flattened his hand as he lowered it, and Brae followed all the way down to the ground. Henry extended his hands in opposite directions, and Brae stretched out his front and back legs until his head and tail were the only parts of him rising above the dirt.

"That was awesome," said Wayne. "Will you show me how to make him do that?"

Henry's outstretched arms shook a little, he was so proud. He tucked them back against his sides.

"Maybe later," said Henry. "C'mon, let's race before the sun comes up."

"It's too dark," said Wayne.

"No it's not."

"My pack is too heavy."

"C'mon!" Henry pulled on Wayne's t-shirt. "Brae's not gonna lie there forever." Brae lifted his head at the mention of his name and looked Henry right in the eyes. "Brae wants you to do it—" Henry flicked his finger in Wayne's direction, and Brae turned his gaze to Wayne.

"Okay, okay," Wayne laughed. "How can I say no to the wonder-dog?"

The boys stood side by side behind Brae, each of them with one foot extended forward, just shy of touching the dog's muddy fur. The trail was flat for a few yards on the other side of the dog. Henry could see that far. And then there was nothing. Just the dark. Probably a steep descent. But just like Henry couldn't see the sun but could feel it, he could feel the mountain too. He and Wayne and Brae belonged there.

"On your mark. Get set. Go!" yelled Henry. And they were off. The boys jumped over Brae and began to run.

* * *

But he'd never do that again. He'd never run on the mountain again. Not with Wayne.

It wasn't going to happen. Ever. Again.

Because here he was, in front of Wayne's casket.

Henry's legs twitched. His breath and heart too. Henry imagined he would twitch and twitch and twitch and explode. A loud bang, and bits of his body would tear off and land all over the church. A hand in an organ pipe. A leg on a pew. His nose on the pulpit, right on the pages of the reverend's open Bible.

"Henry." Mom's voice came through the downpour of body parts. It sounded so far away, but she was right by his side.

Henry didn't answer.

"You can touch him if you want to," Mom whispered.

Henry's arm was outstretched. His hand hovered over the casket. He yanked it back. He didn't want to touch Wayne, he didn't want to look at Wayne, he didn't want to be in this church on this day staring at Wayne, dead. Wayne's mouth was closed, but the corners of his lips were turned up and the middle parts were pushed down so he looked like a stuffed animal. He looked like a stupid stuffed dog that some girl would carry under her arm. He stared at Wayne's mouth searching for thread or glue. Whoever it was that fixed Wayne up had done a real crap job. He must have used Wayne's school picture from last year, because Wayne had made that same stupid face for the photographer. Henry had called him Rover for weeks.

The bottom of Wayne's t-shirt was wrinkled just about where the incision must have been. Henry and Wayne had looked at pictures of dead bodies being embalmed. Now Wayne was embalmed. Wayne's stomach and liver and bladder and guts had all been sucked dry right through that incision. His organs had been filled with some kind of formaldehyde crap. And then he'd been sewn back up and stuffed like a dog. And now Mom wanted Henry to touch him.

Jeezum Crow.

Wayne didn't belong here. He didn't belong here with some sort of weird lipstick on his lips and his hair slicked back with gel, a whacked-out fake dog stuck in a box. Wayne belonged on the mountain.

The treasure box didn't belong here either, but there it was, tucked under Wayne's stiff arm. The brown leather, rubbed through at the hinges from opening and closing the box so many times. Henry remembered talking with Wayne's mother and father, Annie and Jake, about what should go into the casket with Wayne. Annie hadn't wanted to put anything in, but Jake convinced her that the treasure box, and a few treasures, should be with him. Henry just stood there, unable to speak.

Until they put the marble in the box.

Henry had found the extra-big marble on the windowsill in his room when he and Mom moved into their house six years ago. He put it in his pocket, and that was the afternoon he met Wayne. That was the beginning of the luck.

Henry and Wayne traded the marble back and forth after that. Whenever Jake went on a long truck job, Henry gave it to Wayne. Whenever Henry went to visit his own dad, Wayne gave it back to him. If Wayne had a baseball game, he got it. If Henry had a football game, he got it.

Luck for Henry.

Luck for Wayne.

Luck for Henry.

Luck for Wayne.

Now the marble was stuck in the box, stuck in the casket, about to go under the ground, about to be buried forever with Wayne's dead body.

Henry's legs throbbed.

"I have to get out of here," someone said behind him.

Henry turned. It was Jake. His voice sounded too loud for his body.

Mom was now in the back of the church, hugging Annie. The door opened, clapped shut. Jake left. A group of Henry's schoolmates sat on the back of a pew. The reverend picked up hymnbooks.

No one looked at Henry. Or at Wayne. No one.

Henry put his hand in the casket. He opened the treasure box and grabbed the marble between his thumb and fingers. He closed the old leather lid. He touched Wayne's arm—a cold, rubbery arm—and he exploded into a million fiery pieces as he held the marble in his hand. All over—in the organ pipes, the pews, the pages of the open Bible.

Henry clutched the marble. He pulled himself together and ran out of the church.

chapter 3

ZAVION

The street was gone. Just an endless river, rising higher and higher and higher. Crouched in the attic, Zavion wished he could reach up into the sky. Turn off the faucet before the whole world overflowed. But wishing did no good. The world was falling apart.

Zavion couldn't think. He couldn't think of what to do. How could he not think of what to do? That was his job.

The real night had come and gone. Their cereal was gone. Juice, gone. The shingles on the roof of their house cracked and snapped. Zavion watched the dark, rising water suck them down.

"We have to get out of here by ourselves," yelled Papa. His voice was sucked into the wind and rain too. "The house is falling apart." He stared out the window. "Look—"

Water. All Zavion saw was water.

"That—" said Papa, pointing. "I think it's a door."

Zavion strained his eyes and saw something flat racing toward them.

"I'm going to jump onto that door," said Papa, "and then you're going to jump after me. Understand?"

A piece of the window frame tore off the house and plummeted into the water.

Zavion reached to grab Papa's arm. "My room—" he gasped. "My mural. Mama's mural. The mountain—"

Papa didn't seem to hear. He balanced on the ledge of the attic window and jumped. The water was so high that it wasn't far, but Zavion still held his breath until Papa's feet hit the door. It tilted back and forth like a seesaw. Papa grabbed onto a corner of the house to keep the door from rushing down the river.

"Jump!" Papa yelled. Another piece of the window frame tore loose.

Zavion climbed onto the windowsill. He had a strange, strong urge to jump up and grab onto a sheet of rain and pull himself up. Up and up and up.

The wind squealed through the walls of the attic. Long and loud. An entire length of clapboard peeled off the side of the house.

"Zavion!" Papa yelled again. "I can't keep this door still for much longer!" Papa's voice matched the wind. A high-pitched scream. "Jump!"

Zavion closed his eyes. He jumped. He slammed onto the door just as a two-by-four from the attic hit the water next to him. The water splashed hard. The door tipped sharply. Zavion couldn't keep his balance. He slid into the water. The water sucked him down quickly. It coated his skin, cold and slick. Papa's fingers passed over Zavion's arm, his neck, his hair, but Papa couldn't get a hold of him. Papa's hand finally grabbed Zavion's shirt collar. Dragged him alongside the door. Zavion opened his eyes. Black. Dark. Sting. He couldn't touch the bottom, and the rain was coming down so thick and fast it was hard to tell what was river and what was sky. Something firm and long moved across his legs. A snake. Zavion's empty lungs forced his mouth open. He gulped water. Not air. Water. Oily and thick. Papa yanked him back onto the door.

Zavion lay on his back, coughing and spitting thick liquid from his lungs.

"Zavion!" Papa yelled right near his face. "Zavion!"

Zavion turned his head and saw his house—now a small, ragged box in the distance. The two-by-fours holding up the house looked like legs. They buckled at the knees and snapped.

More tiles flew off the collapsing roof, like birds or bats, spinning and crashing into the water.

Zavion grabbed two of the broken slate shingles as they rushed by.

"Papa—"

But Zavion had nothing to say.

"Hands out of the water, Zav," said Papa. "There are snakes in there."

Zavion peered into the water. Water moccasins. He remembered the thick, cold water in his own mouth and shuddered. He looked up instead. The rows of rooftops that were still intact stood like islands. A man and a woman were on top of one, clutching a sign between them. HELP US, it said.

There was nowhere safe to look.

Zavion looked nowhere for what seemed like a long time.

Then Papa said, "We gotta walk now."

The water level was lower here. Zavion didn't remember seeing it go down, but he could tell. The top steps leading up to a few houses were visible.

"Where are we going?" Zavion asked.

"Forward" was all Papa said.

Zavion wanted to walk up, not forward, but he shoved the shingles into his pocket, climbed off the door, and stepped into the waist-high water. Papa grabbed Zavion's hand. The wind tore through their fingers, pulling them apart. As they slogged through the rain and wind, Zavion tried to get his bearings, but nothing looked familiar. Not the sky, not the trees, not the . . . street.

He could barely even remember the word *street*.

It didn't matter. There was no word for what they were walking through now.

chapter 4

HENRY

Henry's legs burned. Good. Pain seared his legs as he turned his bike pedals around and around and around.

Turn, burn. Turn, burn. Turn, burn.

Brae gave up trying to get Henry to leave the driveway and go for a real bike ride; instead, he just loped beside Henry's left leg. Up the long driveway and then back down, turning around and going up, turning around and going down.

At the top of the driveway, Henry stopped. Sweat dripped from his hair and stung his eyes. He didn't want to do it, but Henry couldn't keep from looking at Mount Mansfield. There was nowhere safe to look. The hulking mountain was everywhere. Even through stinging eyes, its edges were sharp, like a picture ripped out of a magazine and pasted against the sky. Henry put his hand in his jeans pocket. He hadn't taken them off since the funeral. Had slept in them. He pulled out the marble. Swirls of blue and green. Flecks of red and orange. He raised it high above his head, hovering over Mount Mansfield like a perfect moon or perfect sun.

But the marble was nothing like perfect. Neither was the mountain. They were both confusing now. They were both dangerous.

Henry shoved the marble back in his pocket. He wiped the hair out of his eyes and pushed off on his bike. Brae let out a yelp.

"Shoot! Sorry, Brae," Henry said. He put his foot on the ground. Brae rested his chin on Henry's knee. "I forgot you were there." Brae stared at him. "I didn't mean to hurt you—"

I didn't mean to hurt you.

Wayne came crashing into Henry's head like a bolt of lightning.

I didn't mean to hurt you.

Wayne, Wayne, Wayne.

Henry squeezed his eyes shut, but he couldn't keep the image from racing in. Wayne's backpack flying down the mountain in front of Henry. Wayne ahead of him in the race. Wayne had longer legs than Henry. Longer strides. Not fair. Henry never beat Wayne.

No, no, no—

Henry's eyes flew open. Brae leaned against the front wheel of his bike. Henry bent down to grip one of his ears. Behind

Brae, against the mountain, Henry saw two flashes of light. What was that? The clouds passing over the sun? Two boys running? Henry was losing his freaking mind. His eyes burned like his legs did. He closed them. He couldn't fight the memory.

Henry finally caught up to Wayne and grabbed at the carabiner hanging from Wayne's backpack. He couldn't quite reach, but Wayne felt him. He turned around, laughing. In that split second, Henry pushed past Wayne. His bare arm rubbed the rough trunk of a pine tree as he made a sharp turn on the trail.

The sun climbed to its feet now, a faint blue light just beginning to spill down on the tree trunks and boulders and ferns. It was so cool the way the sunlight turned everything blue first and then filled in with the rest of the colors. Water on the ferns flashed, like lights on a runway. It was going to be fully sunrise before they were home—Henry knew it. And Mom was going to find out they had spent the night on the mountain, and she was going to be pissed.

Brae jumped over a rock on the side of the trail and landed in front of Henry. He bounded ahead, the black parts of his fur getting lost in the half-light and his white spots reflecting the sun so that he looked like a colony of blue rabbits hopping down the trail. Henry heard a scraping sound behind him and then a grunt.

"You okay, Wayne?" he shouted.

"Yeah," Wayne shouted back.

"Good! I'm leaving you behiiiiiiiind—" Henry jumped from rock to rock to rock, and in those split seconds that he was suspended in the air, in those split seconds that the sun was rising higher and higher, and the world was getting brighter and more full of color, Henry felt like he was making the light.

Henry landed on the trail and kept running. He couldn't hear Wayne's sneakers on the dirt anymore. He'd left him in the dust. Jeezum Crow! That never happened. Brae bounded back up the trail and, at the same time, Henry felt the dirt change to solid rock and then he was at the place where two rock faces met. A wide gap sat between the rocks. He and Brae reached the gap at the same time and they both jumped. Henry's body hung in the air while a surge flowed through him, something warm and fierce, and he felt like he owned the mountain and was a part of the mountain all at the same time.

He landed and pitched forward. He was going to be a part of the mountain, all right. His face was going to be part of a large, hard rock. Shoot! His backpack flung up around his neck and he almost fell face-first, but he grabbed the trunk of a thin pine tree, regained his balance, and kept running.

Maybe he would win the race after all! He'd love rubbing that in Wayne's face.

Bump—

Something jammed him from behind, into the crease behind his knees, and he did fall, his palms smacking against the dirt.

"What the heck, Brae—" Henry's head was bent down, and Brae pushed his long nose under his arm. Henry shoved him back with his elbow. His hands stung like crazy. Brae whined a low, throaty sound.

"What?" Henry looked up.

Brae wiggled out from under Henry's hands and raced back up the trail a few yards, then bounded back again, whining that same awful sound.

Henry's body began to shake. It was Wayne. All of a sudden, he knew it. Something had happened to Wayne.

Again and again, Brae ran up the trail and down again, but Henry was frozen. He was a part of the mountain, like a tree that had grown roots deep into the ground. Henry wasn't sure how many times Brae called for Henry to follow him before Henry yanked himself from the earth and, trembling, ran to the gap and jumped it again to find Wayne.

Henry forced his eyes open. His body was doing it again. His arms and legs and hands and feet were frozen. He couldn't make them move. His bike clattered to the ground.

The bike pedal smashed down on his foot.

"Crap!" he yelled.

He yanked it out from under the pedal and kicked the bike. "Stupid bike," he said. "Stupid mountain. Stupid, stupid, stupid marble."

He jerked the marble from his pocket, ripping the seam, and threw it. The red and orange specks flashed in the sunlight. Like fire. Like magic. Like luck. Then it hit the ground and the magic was gone. What good was it, anyway? It hadn't protected Wayne. It hadn't saved his life.

And it couldn't save Henry anymore.

The marble was crap. It didn't have one speck of luck in it.

Not for him.

Not for Wayne.

Not anymore.

chapter 5

ZAVION

Zavion and Papa were joined by three other people. An older woman held hands with the man and woman on either side of her and kept her eyes closed. She hummed. Zavion could only barely hear her above the roar of the rain as she hummed a low, slow song. Zavion remembered Mama's funeral, and the long walk from the church to the cemetery. There had been a line of people walking then too, and someone had led the group in the same song. "This Little Light of Mine." It had been Mama's favorite, but Zavion didn't sing it that day.

Up, not forward. Up, not forward. Up, not forward. Up, up, up. Zavion chanted this in his head to the rhythm of the grandmama's song.

Up—Up—Up—

If only he could get to higher ground. Solid ground.

For four hours, they slogged through the black water and

pelting rain and tearing wind, and then Zavion saw a small boat paddled by a man in a uniform.

"Looks like a firefighter," Papa said.

When the man got closer, Zavion could see a gun in a holster around his waist.

"Hallelujah," said the man who was holding hands with the grandmama. "Can you get us out of this swamp?"

"Sorry," said the firefighter. "I can't. I want to check to see who all's still stranded behind you."

"You gotta help us," said the woman holding the grandmama's other hand.

"I'm sorry," he said again.

"Take my mama," said the man. "At least take her."

The old woman opened her eyes for the first time then. Zavion saw her look at the firefighter, smile a faint smile, and, humming all the while, close her eyes once again.

"Get yourselves out of here," said the firefighter. "Who knows if the sky will open up again."

Zavion couldn't imagine more water. That thick, oily taste stuck in his mouth.

"Get to the convention center," said the firefighter.

"Which way?" asked Papa.

The firefighter pointed ahead. "Forward."

No—

Up—

Up—Up—Up—

Zavion thought of Mama again. How she had promised to take him to her mountain. Grandmother Mountain. *Up—up—up—to the top.* To see the view. To see where Mama grew up. She had said they would go in the fall, when the monarch butterflies were there.

"Only we'll be migrating north, not south," she'd said.

"I'm sorry," the firefighter repeated. "I'm so sorry." Then he paddled off in the direction of Zavion and Papa's house.

But there was no house.

Zavion felt in his pocket for the shingles. He laid them flat across both palms. Two shingles was all. But it felt as if he was holding his whole house. It had taken Zavion so long to figure out a way to restore balance after Mama died. And now—his whole house teetered there in his shaking, wet hands.

He closed his fingers around the shingles. He felt the hard, smooth slate. But he also felt wood and nails, his bedroom wall and paint too. Home. He felt home precariously balanced in the palms of his hands. Then he stuffed it all back into his pocket and began to walk again.

chapter 6

HENRY

Brae followed Henry up to his room. Henry put his hand in his pocket and touched the marble. Freaking marble. He should have left it outside. Let a bird find it and put it in its nest.

But he didn't.

He couldn't.

He had grabbed it back up.

Henry kicked open his door.

"You scared me!" Mom said.

Henry's clothes were in a big pile on the floor. Some of Wayne's too. Mom folded and stacked them.

"What are you doing?" Henry demanded.

"Did you forget about the clothing drive for the victims of the hurricane?" Mom asked. "I wanted to give some clothes to the drive."

He had forgotten. He grabbed Wayne's red sweatshirt out of Mom's hands.

"Henry—" said Mom.

Out his window, the sun lit Mount Mansfield from behind so that it glowed. Henry's arm shot out. His fist punched the edge of the window frame, a loose joint exploding. Even in his room. Freaking mountain.

"Henry—" Mom said again. "That's not like you—"

Henry rubbed his knuckles. *Shoot, that hurt.*

"You said you wanted to donate some clothes too."

Henry turned around. "I know. But not this." He wrapped the sweatshirt around his throbbing hand.

"It's Wayne's, isn't it?" Mom asked.

Henry hung his head. "Can you just leave?" he said under his breath.

"Why don't you stay home from school again tomorrow, Henry," said Mom. "You're not ready yet."

"Please go."

Mom sighed. "Somehow," she began, "I don't know how, but somehow you're going to be okay." She walked out of Henry's room.

"I will never be okay." Henry sat down on his floor. Brae lay beside him and Henry patted the perfect black circle on the top of his head.

Henry unwrapped the sweatshirt from his hand and laid it flat on the floor. It was much bigger than him. Wayne had been tall and lanky, the perfect size for playing shortstop. He could make a diving lunge for the ball and still throw to first for the out. More of Wayne's clothes lay on the floor. Henry grabbed a pair of sweatpants and a pair of socks. He laid the pants under the sweatshirt and the socks under the pants. He dug under the heap of clothes and found Wayne's Cougars baseball cap, their school team.

"Oh, man." The words were loud and rough coming out of Henry's mouth.

Brae turned his head to see what the fuss was all about.

Henry had built Wayne.

He lay down on the floor on his back, his head almost touching the baseball cap. The night they'd snuck out of the house, they were in sleeping bags at the top of Mount Mansfield. Like this. Head to head. At the top of the world. A billion stars, the two of them and Brae.

Henry sighed. But Brae didn't turn around this time. It wasn't that kind of sound. Instead he curled himself into a ball and settled in, like he had that night on the mountain, for a sleep.

Then both he and Henry, next to the Wayne that Henry had built, closed their eyes.

chapter 7

ZAVION

People filled every inch outside of the convention center. A woman bathed her children out in the open parking lot. Poured bottled water over them. Next to her, a man slept on the concrete. Rested his head on a pillow he had made from the edge of a wooden pallet. People everywhere. Fear everywhere. Zavion could see it. It crawled in every corner of the convention center, leaving footprints over everyone.

Papa pushed his way toward a door. His hand gripped Zavion's arm. The man and woman and grandmama followed them.

"Hey, Zavion, up you get," said Papa.

Zavion hadn't noticed that his legs had buckled underneath him.

"He needs some food," said Papa. "Excuse me, ma'am." He grabbed the arm of a woman who was hurrying out. "Is there food and water inside?"

She was scared. Zavion could see the footprints.

"No," she said. "No, there's no food or water in there." Her voice shook. She hurried away.

"Zavion, stand up," Papa ordered. "We need to find some food."

"We all need some," said the woman holding hands with the grandmama.

"Let's you and I go find something," said the man, pointing to Papa.

"I can't leave him," said Papa.

"He's too tired to walk," said the woman. "Look at him. Leave him with Mama and me."

"I can take care of myself," said Zavion, still on the ground. Feeding himself, feeding Papa, that was his job. He did the food shopping at home. He struggled to stand up. "I'll go," he said. "You all stay here."

"No," said Papa, putting his hands under Zavion's armpits. "You can't even stand on your own. We'll go together." Papa pulled Zavion up onto his feet. "Thank you all, but Zavion is coming with me."

Zavion and Papa walked through water that was only up to their ankles. The word *street* floated back into Zavion's tired mind. They kept walking. The word *block* floated in after *street*. Ten blocks later they found a market. Or the remnants of one. LUNA MARKET, the green and purple sign read. The front window was smashed in. Rows of shelves were tipped over one on top of another like dominoes that had been lined up and knocked down. Papa tried to open the door, but it only moved a few inches. It was blocked by more fallen shelves.

"Over here, Zav," said Papa, leading him back to the broken window.

Papa stepped over the window frame and turned back to take Zavion's hand. Zavion lifted one leg over the frame too, but he was so tired that he lost his balance and jabbed his other leg on the broken glass sticking out from the sill.

Pain shot through him. He moaned without thinking and was immediately ashamed.

"Sweet Jesus," whispered Papa. "Enough is enough, don't you think?" He looked toward the sky.

Yes, thought Zavion.

"Don't move," said Papa. "I'm going to pull."

Zavion held his breath as Papa pulled his leg off the glass.

"I'm sorry," said Zavion.

And he was. He was so sorry. He didn't think he could lose any more control, but it kept happening.

Papa examined the gash. "We need to cover that up," he said. "You don't need an infection on top of everything else."

He tore a strip off his t-shirt and folded it against Zavion's leg, then tore another one and tied it around the makeshift bandage. The gash ached in a steady, pulsing beat.

"Now can you walk?" asked Papa.

Zavion nodded. "Of course."

Papa and Zavion walked through the aisles of the store, stooping under tilted shelves and stepping over spilled food. It looked ransacked, by the hurricane and by humans. Wet boxes of cereal were disintegrated on the ground. Jars of tomato sauce were shattered. Ice cream oozed out of freezer units. The air smelled like sour milk and rotting fruit. Zavion tried to take shallow breaths.

Papa sat on the floor. He closed his eyes and put his head in his hands.

"Papa?" Zavion whispered. He pushed against the t-shirt, and blood seeped through its corner onto his fingers. He wiped his hand across his shirt.

"I don't know what to do." Papa's voice was muffled behind his thick hands. They were clean. No paint on them at all. The floodwater must have taken the paint away. Papa's hands looked naked. In a funny way, Zavion felt embarrassed by them.

Zavion didn't know what do to either. But he had to figure

something out. That was his job. It always had been and he was good at it. He knew how to take care of himself and Papa. Ever since Mama died.

Until now.

Zavion felt heat creep from his neck to his face.

"Papa—" Zavion said it loudly this time. "Papa, I know what to do."

Papa dropped his hands from his face and stared blankly at Zavion—

—who didn't know what to do, not at all.

But he had to.

He had to know—

"Chocolate bars," Zavion said suddenly. "Chocolate bars. They're still safe to eat."

He made his way to the front of the store. Papa followed him. Two candy bar and gum shelves were empty, but one lay on top of the conveyer belt by a cash register. Zavion lifted it. Chocolate bars. He grabbed a handful.

I'm stealing, he thought.

"Let's go," said Papa.

"Wait—"

We need to pay for these. But there's no one here.

"Now," said Papa.

Zavion's thoughts raced. His leg pulsed. His head spun.

We're stealing.

We're surviving.

We're stealing.

Papa walked back toward the broken window. Zavion reached into his pocket and pulled out the two shingles from his roof. The only things he had left in the world. He put them on the checkout counter. A sort of IOU. A record that he had been there and had taken something. A promise that he would be back.

chapter 8

HENRY

Sometime in the middle of the night, Henry woke with a stiff neck and no memory of how he had ended up on the floor. He sat and turned his head from one side to the other. Mount Mansfield glowed in the moonlight and Henry locked eyes with its eyes. His gaze traveled to its forehead, nose, and chin. In his groggy state, the famous face in the mountain looked real.

"Wayne will kick your butt," he said.

Wayne would tackle the mountain to the ground, rip it from the earth, and fling it into space.

But that wasn't going to happen.

Wayne was gone. And the mountain was here to stay.

Henry staggered to his feet. He slid his blue jeans off his tired body and chucked them onto the floor. He made his way to the bed and collapsed. Brae lumbered to his feet and lay down next to the bed. Henry reached his hand down and put it on Brae's belly and felt his muscles vibrate with each breath. But Henry's own body felt still.

Like a corpse.

chapter 9

ZAVION

"Have you tried to go inside?" Papa asked a man standing outside the door to the convention center. He and Zavion couldn't find the man and woman and grandmama to give them some of the chocolate bars.

"No," the man said.

"We shouldn't go in there," said a woman standing next to him. She shook her head and Zavion saw them again. Fear footprints. All across her face.

"Someone saw a boy carrying a knife," she said. She pointed to Zavion. "A boy his age."

"Someone saw a man with his throat slit open. His pockets turned inside out," said the man. "It's the end of the world in there."

"I don't believe it," said Papa. "That firefighter told us to come here. We need to get inside. It's the middle of the night. We have to sleep."

The convention center was overflowing with people. It was hard to walk forward even a few feet. Papa pushed his way farther into the lobby. "It's less crowded just up there," he said over his shoulder. Zavion walked behind him, the sweet taste of stolen chocolate stuck on his tongue. His leg pulsed with a dull ache. His head did too. He just wanted to lie down.

Papa stopped abruptly. He was silent for a moment.

"Sweet Jesus," Zavion heard him whisper under his breath.

"Cover the kid's eyes," said someone in front of Papa.

But it was too late. A woman sat in a wheelchair, slumped forward. A dead woman. Zavion had only ever seen Mama's body, after she died, still and quiet and laid out flat. This body was different. It was puffy. Bent into a strange shape. Like a puppet from a Mardi Gras parade. Zavion hadn't ever seen a body like this, but he knew it was dead.

"No kid should see this," someone else said.

But it didn't matter what he saw. He couldn't escape the smell. The smell of urine. Of sweat. Of death.

Papa turned around then. He pulled Zavion away from the convention center. Away from the boy with the knife. Away from the man with the slit throat. Away from the dead Mardi Gras body. He pulled Zavion away from the parking lot where the man on the pallet tossed and writhed and screamed out in his sleep, away from the man and the woman and the grandmama who hummed "This Little Light of Mine." A gun-shot rang out. Papa pulled and pulled Zavion away from it all, but fear stretched its body long and taut. It followed them. Stepped on their heels.

They walked until they came to the Crescent City Connection Bridge. A soldier, maybe a National Guardsman, turned them around. Told them they couldn't cross the bridge unless they were in a car, and he pointed a gun at them when he said it. So they walked up and down side streets until they found an abandoned car. Papa got in the driver's side and opened the door across from him.

"Survival," he said firmly. Just like he could read Zavion's mind. "Get in."

Survival?

Or stealing?

Zavion couldn't tell the difference anymore.

No, that wasn't exactly true. He could tell the difference, but he couldn't make a choice *based* on the difference. He was so tired.

And then Papa said, "That soldier had a good idea. To find a car. This is a good place to rest. Sleep, son."

Papa locked the car doors and closed his eyes. Zavion closed his eyes too. But fear kept him awake. It padded its small, cold feet up and down his back all night long.

chapter 10
HENRY

Henry woke up sweating and shaking and—wet. The side of his face was wet. Wet, then cold, then wet again, then cold again. When he was finally able to focus his eyes, he saw that Brae was licking his cheek.

He had been dreaming about Wayne.

Henry ran back up the trail. Brae bounded ahead of him a few hundred yards. Henry tried to keep up, but he couldn't. He tripped on a root and fell on his hands again. The sting vibrated like before, only this time it traveled all the way up his arms, into his chest, his neck, his head. He got up, and stumbled again on a muddy rock face. He slammed his elbow and knee hard.

Brae ran back to Henry and licked his cheek and whined a low, throaty sound into his ear. Henry scrambled up and ran and ran and ran. How far back up the mountain was Wayne?

The trail turned right and a rock wall loomed in its path.

Brae sat under it, leaned his head back, and howled like he was trying to set the sun and raise the moon all at once. The sound pierced the sky, and Henry thought the rock wall would crack in two. Brae closed his mouth, took a few steps back, and ran at the wall. He jumped. His front legs reached the top of the rock and his hind legs bicycled in the air until he got a foothold. Henry climbed up after him.

The trail turned left and opened into treetops and exposed rock. The fog had settled down thick, and Henry couldn't see far ahead. When had the fog come? Brae disappeared and reappeared, like a magic trick, as he ran up the trail, then doubled back to check on Henry. Brae here, Brae gone, Brae here, Brae gone. But the fog remained, like Henry's fear, heavy and gray and everywhere.

Brae stopped. He inched over to the edge of the rock. He whimpered. Henry's feet slowed down. His heart sped up. Oh crap. Oh crap, crap, crap. Had Wayne fallen over the edge of the rock? They had peered over that rock ledge a million times before. It was a sharp drop and there was rock at the bottom, but it wasn't very far down. Henry knelt, his hands still stinging, and crawled up to the edge. The fog followed him.

Wayne.

Henry's heartbeat sped up again and thumped out his best friend's name.

Wayne. Wayne Wayne. Wayne Wayne Wayne Wayne Wayne.

Brae whined and pushed his cold nose under Henry's hand. Had Henry just said Wayne's name out loud? Henry sat up in bed and swung his feet to the floor. The wood was freezing, and he buried his toes into the thick fur on Brae's warm back.

"You up?" Mom's voice came from the kitchen.

"Yeah!" Henry yelled back. He slid his feet onto either side of Brae and sat like he was on a black and white horse. Brae was that big. When people asked Henry what breed he was, he always said part Border collie, part Holstein cow.

A knock at the door. "Henry," came Mom's voice. Jeez, hadn't she heard him? She walked in.

"How many times are you just gonna walk into my room without asking me?"

"How did you sleep?" Mom tried to brush Henry's hair from his face, but he pushed her hand away.

"Like crap."

"Me too. I kept thinking about all those families in that hurricane. Can you imagine? Your house floating in tiny pieces down the street? You floating down the street with it? Can you imagine if that were you, Henry?"

What if Henry had lost his home and was rowing a boat

that used to be his dresser drawer? What if he was careening down a river that used to be his street? He didn't want to play a dumb *What If* game with Mom. He had enough of his own *What If*s to keep him busy. *What if* Henry and Wayne had stayed home that night? *What if* they hadn't raced? *What if* he had been able to save Wayne?

"*What if* that was me in the hurricane?" said Henry. He put his hands on Brae's head and pulled his ears. "I'd ride Brae like he was a dolphin until I hit dry land," he said, jumping up from the bed and pushing past Mom. "I gotta get ready for school."

chapter 11

ZAVION

In the morning, Papa and Zavion walked back toward the Crescent City Connection Bridge.

"I wish there had been keys in that car," said Papa.

"You wanted to steal it?" Zavion asked. "We haven't repaid the store for the chocolate bars, and you wanted to steal a car?" He rubbed his eyes hard, hoping when he opened them again that he would blink a few times and find himself home in his bed.

"We'd have borrowed it, Zav," said Papa as he lifted his hand to flag down a van. But it drove by them. "If the keys had been in the console, I would have taken it as a sign."

A sign that Zavion wasn't home in bed.

Borrowing, surviving—Papa had all these words for it, but it was still stealing.

The early sun burned the fog off the river and out of Zavion's gut. Survival sizzled and popped and disappeared, and stealing remained in the bright light.

Zavion had argued this point with Papa plenty of times before. Papa would grab a paint can out from in front of someone's house without asking and not feel one ounce of worry that the person might not be finished with it. It drove Zavion crazy. How could he be absolutely sure? It was only a few weeks into the school year and Zavion had already asked his teacher twice if *thinking about* looking at someone's paper was the same as looking at it. His teacher had said no, but it still left Zavion feeling unsettled, knowing that he had the potential to look because he had an idea of it in his brain.

A pickup truck pulled up next to them. A man leaned across the seat toward the open window on the passenger side. He wore a New Orleans Saints baseball hat. "Need a ride?" he asked.

"Yes," said Papa.

"Hop in." The man pushed the truck door open.

"Go on, Zav," said Papa.

"We shouldn't do this," said Zavion. "We don't know him."

"We have to get out of New Orleans, and I can't paint my way out."

Zavion had a flash of one of Papa's brightly colored canvases stretched across the bridge. Walking on the hands of trumpet-playing musicians from one side to the other. He blinked and had another flash of the mural in his room. Grandmother

Mountain. Mama's mountain. Mama had promised to show Zavion where she had lived until she met Papa, to take him to meet Grandmother Mountain someday. He couldn't walk across the river on that mural, but maybe he could climb it to the sky.

He wanted to climb it—

"Get in." Papa interrupted Zavion's thoughts. "We need to get across this bridge."

Zavion climbed into the truck. A black canvas bag sat in the middle of the seat.

"Sorry," said the man. "You can just shove that over."

Papa extended his hand across Zavion. "I'm Ben," he said.

"Joe," said the man.

"And this is Zavion. Thank you for the ride."

"No problem. I've been traveling back and forth for the last two days, giving folk rides when I can." Joe started the truck up again and began to drive toward the bridge. "How can they not let people across on foot, you know? It's just not right." He shook his head.

"What do you do?" asked Papa. Zavion wondered the same thing.

"I'm a photojournalist," said Joe.

Zavion looked at the bag next to him. "Is this your camera?" he asked.

"One of them, yup."

Zavion wondered what kinds of pictures were in the camera. Were there any from his neighborhood? Or his block? Was there a picture of his house?

Joe slowed the truck down as they approached an official-looking man, maybe another National Guardsman, stationed at the bridge. Joe rolled down his window. "Good morning," he said.

"Morning," said the man. "Where you off to?"

Papa leaned over Zavion. "Baton Rouge," he said without hesitation. "To my friend Skeet's house."

When had Papa thought of that idea?

"He knows you're coming?" asked the man.

"Yes," said Papa.

Stealing—and now lying. The words glared shiny and bright in Zavion's gut. What if the man pulled out a phone to check on Papa's story? Zavion held his breath and felt his heart beating in the center of his throat.

"This is your truck?" the man asked Joe.

"Yes," he said.

"These are your friends?"

Beat—Beat—Beat—

Up—Up—Up—

Just like Zavion wanted to climb a mountain, his heart wanted to climb out of his mouth.

"Yup," said Joe.

The man gave a slight nod. "Have a good day," he said.

Joe rolled up the window.

"We're going to Skeet's?" Zavion asked when they got to the other side of the bridge.

"I thought of it this morning," said Papa. "Maybe he can help us out. Is there a way to get to Baton Rouge from here?" he asked Joe.

"Yeah," said Joe. "You take I90 to 3127 and then cross the Sunshine Bridge." He pulled a phone out of his shirt pocket. "Here," he said. "You want to call your friend?"

While Papa made the call, Zavion looked out at the Mississippi River and imagined Grandmother Mountain rising up from its watery bottom. What if she had traveled all the way to Louisiana? That was the story that Mama always told, that Grandmother Mountain had been a wanderer. She would trek to a valley, stay for a while, but then get restless and move on. Maybe to a stream, or a forest, or a river.

What if she hadn't settled in North Carolina, but had lumbered farther south, to right here? Zavion's heart raced along with his thoughts. If Grandmother Mountain had put down her roots in the Mississippi River, Zavion could climb her all the way to the top.

He squeezed his eyes shut and wished wished wished that

when he opened them he would see red spruce trees reaching toward the sky.

But when he opened his eyes, Grandmother Mountain was nowhere to be seen.

The Mississippi River stretched into forever.

Zavion's guilt stretched right along with it. He had stolen those chocolate bars. He had. Zavion himself. The one who prided himself on Taking Care Of, and Looking Out For, and Being In Control.

And now—

He was ashamed. He was Letting People Down, Making Bad Decisions, and—

Out.

Of.

Control.

His knee began to shake wildly. He couldn't make it stop.

His house was gone. His things were gone. There was rain. There was too much rain. There was a dead body. Images flew through Zavion's mind like he was running a race. He needed to stop them. He needed to focus.

On one thing.

Now.

How was he going to repay Luna Market?

chapter 12
HENRY

There was no way Henry was going to school. He couldn't face anyone there. He wouldn't be able to concentrate in math on percentages, or in science about solids and liquids.

On instinct he headed for Wayne's house.

The middle of the trail between Henry and Wayne's went through a red pine grove. It was like walking on an old carpet. Henry's boots stopped snapping and shuffling, and he could hear the birds chasing after the wind, and the squirrels scraping their claws up and down the bark of the trees. He always loved this place, the quietest place on earth, the place that brought him straight to Wayne's.

"Out of the way!" a voice screamed from behind him.

Okay, not quiet today.

Henry jumped, Brae jumped, and Henry swore the trees jumped too. He turned around. His up-the-hill neighbor, Nopie Lyons, bombed down the trail on his bike. His hair was in his eyes, a huge backpack pushed his chest onto the bike frame, and silver boots came up over his pants. He looked like a cross between a turtle and an electric mixer. Nopie was a freak of nature, and he was coming straight at Henry.

Henry dove out of the way just in time.

"You're going the wrong way for school, Nopie!" Henry yelled as Nopie sped away.

Brae loped after Nopie.

"C'mon, Brae," called Henry. "Stay with me." He remembered the last time he had seen Nopie. The time before the funeral. "Please stay with me."

chapter 13

ZAVION

"**Does it have a bathroom?**" Zavion leaned over to whisper to Papa.

Joe had driven them over the Sunshine Bridge and Skeet had picked them up and brought them the rest of the way here.

"Of course it has a bathroom. Two of them. And good water pressure too," came a loud voice from above their heads.

A strong, minty smell came along with it. Not the sweet smell of gum or peppermint candy, but the sharp, fresh smell of real mint. Zavion turned his head. A woman with thick glasses, long gray dreadlocks, and knitting needles in her hands leaned over the railing of the stairs behind him. The needles were moving fast. A long scarf dangled by her side.

"The bathrooms are both blue," she said. "Very soothing. Easy to be in there when you have to do your business."

"You remember Ms. Cyn, Ben?" said Skeet.

"Of course. Hello, Ms. Cyn," said Papa. He stood on his toes to give the woman a kiss on the cheek.

"Hello, Ben," Ms. Cyn said, tapping Papa on the nose with her knitting needles and continuing down the stairs.

Zavion looked around the room. Sleeping bags covered the floor and the two couches and even a chair. The walls were bare except for a large cloth banner of a boy sitting at the base of a tree reading a book. Just above his lap, another book floated open in the air. And above that, where the branches started in the tree, a sort of half-book, half-bird floated again. Then, finally, a bird, wings outstretched, flew high in the sky. Written across the tree, in letters that sat hanging from the branches like fruit, was the word *gratitude*.

Zavion recognized the painting style. The banner was one of Skeet's.

How cool would it be to jump into the banner? To be the book? To jump, fly, up, up, turn into a book-bird, fly some more, higher and higher, until he was a real bird, wings wide, soaring in the sky?

"You ever been in Baton Rouge before?" Ms. Cyn asked Zavion, interrupting his thoughts. She motioned for him to sit with her on the bench at the bottom of the stairs. She knit and chewed her mint leaves.

"No, ma'am," Zavion said. He scanned the room. Skeet and

Papa knelt on the floor with two men who Zavion didn't recognize. They were playing some sort of game with marbles. A little girl played on the rug near them.

"Well, welcome, then."

"Thank you, ma'am."

"You gonna tell me your name?"

"Oh. Yes, ma'am," said Zavion. "My name is Zavion."

"Don't think I didn't already know it, Zavion," said Ms. Cyn, and she laughed a deep, loud laugh.

Ms. Cyn's needles flew in and out of the scarf. She reached into her pocket and pulled out a strip of yellow cloth. It was soft, like a piece of an old t-shirt. Zavion watched as she knit the cloth right into the scarf.

"What'd you do that for?" Zavion asked.

"What did I do?"

"That piece of cloth. Why'd you put it into the scarf?"

"I did it there too. See?"

Ms. Cyn pointed one of her needles to another strip of cloth toward the bottom of the scarf. A dark orange rectangle, hard to see because the wool was almost the same color.

"But what are they?"

"That orange one down at the bottom is from Tavius's t-shirt. And the yellow one here is from a shirt of Isaac's. A little bit of family for wrapping around someone's scrawny neck." The girl came running over to them. "A chicken neck just like this one. This is my grandniece, Osprey," said Ms. Cyn, pulling on one of her pigtails. "Osprey, this is Zavion."

"How old are you?" Osprey asked.

"Um—ten," said Zavion.

"I'm four," she said. "My dog, Crow, died in the hurricane. This was his leash." She held a purple nylon leash in her hand.

"Hush," said Ms. Cyn. She patted Osprey on the cheek. "Don't let her sweet face sucker you. She's fierce as a tiger."

Zavion glanced back at the banner. The boy under the tree looked a little like Osprey. Osprey ran back to the rug to play.

"And those three clowns playing Ringer on the floor with your Papa—that one is Skeet, but you know him. He owns this house, and he was married to my daughter, God rest her soul, she died two years ago. Those are his two brothers, Enzo and Tavius. Enzo is Osprey's daddy. They escaped New Orleans like you." Ms. Cyn took a deep breath. "And me. The only other person you need to know is me, Ms. Cyn. The Queen of Baton Rouge." Ms. Cyn laughed a deep, minty laugh.

Zavion tried to repeat these new names inside his head, but pictures raced through it instead. His house. The water. The roof shingles. Luna Market. Chocolate bars. Rain.

"Go on into that blue bathroom, Zavion," said Ms. Cyn.

"Change your shirt. Change your pants." She pointed her knitting needle at Zavion's sleeve. Blood was splattered across it. He hadn't even noticed.

"I cut my leg—" he mumbled.

"Tavius!" Ms. Cyn yelled to one of the men on the floor.

"Yes, ma'am?"

"Get this boy, Zavion, some new clothes."

Tavius reached behind a couch and pulled out a plastic bag. "Here!" he yelled to Zavion, tossing the bag.

"Thank you," said Zavion.

"We got first pick at the Salvation Army."

"How come we got first pick?" teased Enzo.

"Is it 'cause Pierre has a crush on you?" Skeet knocked his shoulder into Tavius's shoulder.

Tavius grinned.

"Go wash out that cut, Zavion. There's first aid cream in the bathroom," said Ms. Cyn.

Zavion managed to stand. Walk across the room. He pushed open the bathroom door and fell against it as it closed. He jumped. Something moved up his back. He turned to look, but nothing was on the door. Whatever it was moved under his t-shirt. Crawled on his skin. He reached his hand through the neck of his shirt to his shoulder. His hand swept from shoulder blade to shoulder blade. Nothing was there. But still, he felt it.

Felt it. Heard it. Smelled it. Tasted it.

He pulled his hand back out of his t-shirt.

Zavion couldn't move. He couldn't even get out of the bathroom and back to the bench.

Instead, he gripped the bathroom door so hard his forearm shook—the rain pouring, the men shooting marbles and laughing, the water rising, the little girl playing, his mural breaking, Grandmother Mountain crumbling, his house collapsing, Ms. Cyn knitting, and the wind—the wind whipping and pulling and pushing him. His knees buckled and he fell to the floor. He couldn't keep his balance in the middle of it all.

chapter 14

HENRY

"The school secretary didn't mention there was a field trip to our house today," said Jake. "And on the second day of school too." He sat next to Nopie, drinking a cup of coffee.

Nopie was at the table!

Henry couldn't believe it. But there he was, hunched over a piece of paper, drawing something. A heat rose up inside Henry. A smoky heat that curled and wisped from his feet all the way to his face. What was Nopie doing here, just sitting all comfortable, in Henry's chair, the chair Henry had sat in a million times before with Wayne right next to him, like he belonged there?

Nopie's head shot up all of a sudden like a spark had singed his eyebrow, and he grabbed hold of a Tupperware container full of something white.

"My mom needed some sugar," Nopie said. "She's making an apple pie for Pop and she ran out of sugar and when we went apple picking the other day we got a whole lot of those tart apples, 'cause it's really too early to pick apples, the kind that make your eyes water when you bite into them, so she really needs the sugar to sweeten 'em up and—"

"Give it a rest, Nopie," said Henry. "Your mouth is gonna fall off."

"Henry . . ." Annie cut the bottoms off some flower stems. She shot Henry a look.

"So I came here to get sugar," Nopie finished, and took in a deep breath.

"Great," said Henry. He put his hand out to pat Brae, but Brae lumbered over to Nopie and wagged his whole body against his shiny, silver-booted leg.

Nopie sat there, shaking the sugar container like it was a maraca. He had lived up the road from Henry for as long as Henry could remember. His motor mouth was the most glaring thing about him, always talking a mile a minute like he had lost the brakes on his tongue. But there was other weird stuff about him too. Like Nopie kept a rabbit at the school all last year in the lighting booth in the school auditorium. He had stolen a key from the janitor. Henry had to admit that was pretty impressive, but still, Nopie was a grade-A weirdo electric mixer–turtle dude.

"Sit down, Henry," said Annie. "I'll make you boys something to eat."

Henry didn't want to eat. He thought if he managed to swallow anything it would end up charred in his belly.

"So which neighbor saw Tiger last?" Nopie interrupted Henry's thoughts.

"Four neighbors said they saw him," said Annie. "I think the last one was Mack."

"I'm making a map of all the houses on the road and then marking where Tiger's been spotted," Nopie said to Henry.

"Good for you."

Jake put down his coffee. "Tiger's been gone since the day Wayne died." His leg began to bounce up and down under the table.

"He used to take walks with me," said Annie. She brought a plate of apples and peanut butter to the table. "Like a dog. He would follow me onto the trail and walk the whole thing at my side. Honestly."

"Tiger is a strange cat," said Nopie.

"You're strange," said Henry.

"*Was* a strange cat," said Jake. "Maybe a fisher's gotten him."

"Don't say that, Jake," said Annie.

Tiger could not be gone. *Oh man*, all the wrong things were disappearing—Henry glared at Nopie—and all the wrong things were staying rooted right where they were.

Nopie chewed on his apple, sucking peanut butter from

between his teeth. Henry focused on that. Henry couldn't decide which was a worse sound: the chewing-sucking one or the Nopie-running-his-mouth one.

"See," said Nopie, his tongue thick with peanut butter—*great*, Henry was going to be serenaded by *both* sounds, "the four neighbors who saw Tiger are all on the same side of the road." He pointed to his drawing. "One, two, three, four . . . all of them heading up to Mansfield." Nopie paused. "Maybe he's looking for Wayne."

Jake's bouncing leg got faster.

"Animals get sad when their owners leave them," said Nopie. He leaned way down and put his arms around Brae's neck. Henry's whole body stiffened. Brae licked the peanut butter off the corners of Nopie's mouth.

Annie filled a jar with water and put a handful of flowers in it. "There was an interview on the radio this morning with a man who had to leave his dog behind when he escaped the hurricane. And he was sure that the dog had died." Annie plucked a flower out of the jar and held it up to her nose. "But he was wrong. The dog escaped from the house, swam through the flooded streets, and found him."

Jake's leg doubled its speed. The table wiggled as his knee hit it from underneath.

"Animal navigation," said Nopie. "Like homing pigeons. Scientists don't know how they can find their way back home."

"That's what they said about this dog," said Annie. "They don't know how he got out of the house or how he smelled the man with the water washing over everything, but he found him."

"Animals have an extrasensory perception," said Nopie. "I bet Tiger feels something strong about Wayne, and he's looking for him."

"Ah!" Jake pulled his hand away from his coffee mug. "Shoot! I burned myself!" He rubbed his knuckles with his other hand.

"I wonder if Tiger knows that Wayne died," said Nopie. "I bet he doesn't—"

Jake stood up suddenly and almost knocked over the table. Nopie's pencil fell to the floor.

"I'm going to New Orleans," he said.

"*Perro*," said Annie.

"Pardon me?" said Jake.

"Isn't that the Spanish word for *dog*?" said Annie.

"Yes," said Henry. "We learned the names of animals in Spanish class. *Perro*. Dog. *Gato*. Cat. *Pájaro*. Bird."

"I've been thinking—I want to learn Spanish."

"Did you hear me?" said Jake. "I'm going to New Orleans—" Jake stumbled around his words. "Early Saturday morning," he said with clarity. "Before the sun comes up."

"There's more French in New Orleans, isn't there?" said Annie. "Not as much Spanish?"

"Annie?" Jake asked her name like a question.

"I understand," she sighed. "You're going to New Orleans."

"They still need folks to drive truckloads of food and clothes. I'll only be down there for a few days. I need to go." Jake walked to the kitchen door but then turned around. "I'll be sad to miss that apple pie, Nopie."

Nopie looked up from his drawing. "I'll freeze you a piece," he said solemnly.

Jeez, what a stupid thing to say.

"I'll be back to eat it," said Jake. He turned and walked out.

For a long time, Henry and Nopie and Annie sat at the table and stared at the flowers in the jar. Henry watched their petals brighten and dim as clouds passed over the sun again and again, then looked outside the window at Jake fiddling under the hood of his rig. The big, shiny green eighteen-wheeler brightened and dimmed too, and the heat inside Henry slowly burned down, until all that was left were flickering embers—on and off, on and off—barely lighting the darkness inside his body.

chapter 15

ZAVION

Water was filling up his mouth again.

And his nose.

And his ears.

Rain clattered from every direction.

His arms windmilled, frantic.

He opened his eyes.

He had been trying to swim up for air, but air was all around him.

Zavion willed his heart to slow down by counting his breaths in and counting his breaths out. His eyes darted around the strange room until he remembered where he was.

He had no idea if it was morning or afternoon or night.

And where was everyone else?

Zavion walked through the door that separated the living room from the kitchen. Ms. Cyn was in blue jeans and a t-shirt, her long gray dreadlocks tied back in a scarf, standing in front of a big cutting board.

"Do you need some help?" Zavion asked.

She whipped around so fast her hair slapped her in the face.

"Lordy, child!" she said. "You scared the living pee out of me!"

One of her dreadlocks had stuck to a piece of dough that was on her face, just hanging there, like it was glued on.

The skin around her eyes folded into wrinkle marks and she laughed.

"Did you have a good nap? No one had the heart to wake you."

No, thought Zavion. He didn't think he'd ever sleep well again.

"What time is it?" he said.

"A little after two. You wanna take over making this bread?" Ms. Cyn asked. "Here's a secret." She leaned in toward Zavion. "I despise cooking." She said the word *despise* like it was two words. *Deeee Spies.* "And if I'm going to let you be witness to the whole truth, Zavion, honey, I despise the very kitchen itself. There, I said it. Amen."

Zavion stood staring at the bread dough.

"It doesn't like me, but it won't bite you," she said. "Go on."

He wrapped his hands on either side of the dough. It was warm. He squeezed so it rose up.

"Push on it," said Ms. Cyn.

It was stiff. Zavion got up onto his knees on the stool in front of him so he could put his whole body into it.

"That's right," said Ms. Cyn. She stood behind him and put her hands on his hands. "Now turn it, fold it, and push again. It's called kneading," she said. "And look at that. You're hired."

Push the dough, then turn it, fold it, and then push again.

He grabbed the rhythm like it was a life preserver.

"How many times do I knead it?" said Zavion.

"You'll feel it get more elastic," said Ms. Cyn.

"How many times?" he asked again.

"Maybe forty or fifty times."

"Forty-five?"

"Yes, child. Forty-five." Ms. Cyn took Zavion's shoulder and gently turned him toward her. "Do you know what you're doing right there?" she said. Her eyes were shiny. Zavion shook his head. "You're making gluten."

"What's gluten?"

"It's a protein that keeps the bread from falling apart." She looked like she was about to cry. "It also helps create little air pockets that let the dough rise on up."

Zavion liked the sound of that.

Ms. Cyn shook her head and clapped her hands. "How's that gash on your leg healing?" she said. "May I?" She knelt down and pulled up his pant leg. "Nicely. Good."

The kitchen door opened.

Osprey walked in wearing high-heeled sandals, a scarf, and large, round sunglasses. She was holding on to a leash attached to a watering can.

"*Good morning to you! Good morning to you!*" she sang. "*Good morning, dear—*" She paused and pulled her sunglasses up onto her head. "*Good morning, dear new boy who I forget the name of! Good morning to you!*"

"Uh—it's not morning," Zavion said.

"But that's how the song goes." Osprey pulled her sunglasses to the edge of her nose and stared at Zavion. "What's your name again?"

"Zavion."

"Well, Zavion, this is Flower." She pointed to the watering can. "You have a pet?" said Osprey. She did a somersault on the kitchen floor. "A dog?"

"No," said Zavion.

"I had a dog," said Osprey. She spun in circles around Zavion's stool. "I'm still teaching Flower how to do tricks, but my dog, Crow, he knew how to do all of them. He could roll over.

He could sit with a piece of food on his nose and then flip it up in the air and eat it. He could play dead." Osprey was making Zavion dizzy. "Now he's dead all the time." She stopped spinning and flopped on the floor.

Ms. Cyn grabbed up Osprey and hugged her tight. "You hungry, little glamour girl?" She kissed each of the lenses on Osprey's sunglasses. Osprey giggled.

The kitchen door opened again.

"Dinner would be ready sooner if your Grand-Auntie Cyn had done her job," said Enzo, leaning into the kitchen.

"Hello to you too," said Ms. Cyn.

"You'd think the floor was made of snakes the way you're afraid to step foot in this kitchen here," said Enzo.

Zavion flinched. Water moccasins. In his kitchen.

"Now, you hush—" said Ms. Cyn.

"Come on outside and play with me, little angel girl," said Enzo.

Osprey wiggled her way out of Ms. Cyn's arms. "I gotta go take Flower out to pee and then we can play," she said as she skipped out of the kitchen, dragging the watering can behind her.

Push the dough, then turn it, fold it, and then push again.

Twenty-nine.

Thirty.

Thirty-one—

And then rain.

Pouring down hard.

Zavion jumped off his stool.

All of a sudden, when his heart beat, it hurt.

The pain was unbearable.

Ms. Cyn rushed to his side.

She made a soft, clicking sound with her tongue against her teeth.

"It was just the sprayer on the kitchen sink," she whispered. "Foolish of me."

This time she was crying.

Papa came in as Zavion began to knead again.

"This is a regular diner, all these people coming and going," said Ms. Cyn. "Hello, Ben."

"Any chance for some coffee?" Papa asked in his gravelly voice.

Ms. Cyn held up a mug. "Yah, Ben. Right here." She poured coffee from the metal carafe and handed it to him.

"Bless you," he said. "Move over, Zavion." Papa sat on the

stool as Zavion pushed the cutting board and bread dough out of the way and hopped up onto the counter.

"We have to figure out where we're going," said Papa.

Zavion sat the bread dough in his lap and squeezed it again. It rose up between his fingers like a mountain. He thought of Grandmother Mountain. That's where they needed to be.

"We should go to a mountain."

Papa reached up to tousle Zavion's hair.

"Hey, are you getting paint in my hair?" Zavion asked, ducking out of the way. Papa had a slash of green paint across his hand. Leave it to Papa to somehow find a canvas when everything else was lost. "So what about a mountain, Papa?" said Zavion. He wiggled his legs. He was going to have flour all over the seat of his pants.

"What about it?"

"Can we go there?" Zavion asked.

"What do you mean, *there*? Just find some mountain? And what—live in a cave?"

"Can we go to Grandmother Mountain? Like Mama promised?"

Zavion saw Papa flinch. It was a tiny movement, a small ripple under his eyes. "I'm thinking we'll go move near Gabe."

"I don't know Gabe," Zavion said, his heart sinking. He had only ever met his uncle once.

"Well, it's high time you did know him, then, don't you think?" Papa said.

"You almost done with the breads, honey?" Ms. Cyn winked at Zavion.

"Almost," he said.

"You're making bread?" said Papa, raising his head.

"He's good at it," said Ms. Cyn.

"He cooks at home too—or, uh—cooked." Papa paused. "I'll bet he's good at it. Let me get out of here so you can finish."

"But, Papa—"

"Zavion's a responsible boy," said Ms. Cyn. She put a hand on Zavion's shoulder as she said *boy*, like she was reminding Papa of something.

"He's a good boy." Papa walked to the door. Then he turned back. "We'll figure this out, Zav."

Zavion brushed flour off his pants and got back down onto the stool. He already had it figured out. They were going to Grandmother Mountain. That was the plan.

He kneaded the dough fourteen more times. There was that funny feeling again—like some creature crawling under his shirt. He pulled his hands out of the dough and scratched the base of his neck. "I think I'm done," he said.

Ms. Cyn stretched a corner of the dough into a thin rectangle. "Perfect," she said. "See that? The thin sheet? See how it doesn't break? That means it's ready to rise. You're a natural. Now break the dough into two sections and shape them into rounds," said Ms. Cyn, handing Zavion a wooden paddle with a long handle. "Put them on this, okay? Then all you do is wait and let them rise."

Let them rise.

Zavion liked the sound of that.

chapter 16

HENRY

Henry sat at the base of the big pine tree behind his house. School was only just out, he figured, and he didn't want to go inside until Mom was back fom her errand.

He'd never cut before. Wayne had, and he'd tried to get Henry to do it with him, but Henry had been too scared. He'd felt a funny feeling in his belly like he did on Valentine's Day, the one holiday his dad sent him anything, a crazy-ton of candy that he always ate before breakfast. Just thinking about cutting made him feel that way, so he couldn't imagine what it would feel like to actually do it.

One time Wayne wanted him to cut school so they could climb Mount Mansfield and spend the whole day up there. Henry had been tempted to say yes, but Brae had sat down between them, looked up at Henry, and yowled. Brae kept Henry on the straight and narrow. But Wayne had begged him so hard and for so long that Henry finally suggested they leave really early one weekend morning and spend the day on the mountain. Wayne said that was boring, but what if they slept up there one night? And even though Henry had felt a little of that candy-in-the-belly feeling, he swallowed it down and said he'd ask Mom. Wayne said no, that he wanted to sneak out of the house one night and do it, and the sickly sweet feeling got bigger, and so Henry said no, but Wayne grabbed the idea between his teeth like Brae with a bone and he wouldn't let go.

Brae had been taking a nap at the time or he wouldn't have ever let Henry agree to the plan.

Wayne had sealed the deal. "It's your turn with the marble," he said. "You've got the luck. Nothing's gonna happen. We won't get caught."

Henry had felt in his pocket, felt the cool, smooth curve of the marble, and that was when he'd said, "Okay, let's do it."

Henry stared up at Mansfield from under the pine tree. He would never, ever get out from under the accusing fingers and glares pointed right at him. Every single tree and rock blamed him, and every stream shouted *you did this, you did this, you did this* as they flowed down the mountain. He could see Mansfield from every window in his house.

Mom pulled into the driveway. Henry waited until she'd gone inside, and then he walked around the house to the front door and let himself in.

"How was school?" Mom called from the kitchen.

"Fine."

Mom came into the mudroom. "Was it really? You didn't have to go, you know—I was worried—but then I thought it might feel better to be there—"

"I said it was fine," said Henry sharply.

Mom put her hand on Henry's cheek. "Okay, okay," she said quietly. And then she changed the subject. "I brought the clothes to the police station," she said brightly.

Henry pulled himself away from Mom. "What clothes?"

"Don't worry," Mom said. "I didn't take Wayne's."

"Which ones did you take?" Henry ran for the stairs.

"The ones on the floor," Mom called after him.

Henry flew into his room. The Wayne he had built was still lying on his floor. But the rest of the clothes were gone. Including his blue jeans.

With the marble in the pocket.

Henry yanked open his dresser drawer. Maybe Mom had put the jeans back. He threw sweatpants and shorts and corduroys on the floor. No blue jeans.

"What are you looking for?" Mom had followed Henry up the stairs.

"My blue jeans! Where are my blue jeans?"

"I gave them away."

"But I wear them, Mom!"

"They were too big. I don't know why your father bought them for you. He is a grown man and he keeps thinking that he's going to grow taller than five foot eight. He's not. And you're not. You were never going to grow into them."

"They were mine, Mom!" Henry got close to her face. "I wore them! I liked them! You had no right to give them away!"

"I'll buy you another pair."

"I don't want another pair!" Henry's belly felt worse than on Valentine's Day morning. "Take me to the police station now! I need to get those blue jeans back!"

"Henry, calm down—" Mom put her hands on Henry's shoulders. He ducked down out of her grip and walked away. "We can't go get them. They're on the highway by now, honey, heading to New Orleans—"

The marble.

It was gone.

Henry had wanted to throw it into the woods, had wanted to get rid of it, but he hadn't. He couldn't. He had kept it. And now it was in his jeans pocket, in a garbage bag, in a truck, speeding away down the highway.

MARGARITA MONTERO

Margarita turned the radio down so she could hear better.

"Marco did what?" she asked into the phone. She couldn't have heard Christo right. "He scored a goal?" She couldn't believe it. How many hours had she and Christo spent in the backyard with Marco, showing him how to dribble, showing him the sweet spot on the side of his sneaker, taking turns standing in the goal as Marco shot soccer ball after soccer ball to the outside of the metal posts?

In this case it was like mother, like son. When Margarita had been five—no, maybe it was even earlier, like age four or even three—her father had taken her to the park almost every day to practice goal kicks. Margarita remembered him leaning against the white post, his hair back in a ponytail, smoking a cigarette, shaking his head, disappointed as she missed every goal.

At home, in Spain, everyone played soccer. Margarita's

father played, her older brother, even her two younger step-brothers played. It was expected that Margarita would too. But she didn't want to. Her feet had no interest—or her feet had no skill—in kicking the ball, and her fingers always itched to fit themselves around the markers she had under her bed in her room. The ones her *abuela* had given her. She spent hours pulling the markers out of their plastic sleeve and rearranging their order.

Rainbow order—*rojo, anaranjado, amarillo, verde, azul, púrpura.*

Complementary order—*rojo y verde, anaranjado y azul, amarillo y púrpura.*

Favorite color order—*púrpura, verde, anaranjado, azul, amarillo, rojo.*

Margarita pulled her hand away from her ear to adjust the rearview mirror. She could barely see with all the garbage bags piled up in the back of the truck. She grinned. It felt good to be doing something useful. Taking these clothes to the kids down in New Orleans. Almost a year in Vermont now, and she was still trying to find a teaching job. She put the phone back to her ear. She had missed some of what Christo had said.

"Yes, I promise. I'll let you know when I get there. I love you and Marco too," she said. "Oh, and tell Marco I challenge him to kick a goal past me when I get home." She clicked off her phone.

Margarita stretched her neck from one side to the other and saw a small green car pass her on the left. Two little kids were in the backseat, their heads close together, hunched over something, maybe playing a game. She checked the truck clock. 6:14 p.m. She decided she'd drive as far as she could. Until she began to experience that almost-asleep feeling. The truck driver at the Williston Police Department had left her with that one piece of advice.

"Stop driving as soon as you feel your eyelids get heavy. Even if it's for a half second. Those half seconds can turn into seconds, and then those seconds can turn into sleep really fast," he had said.

Margarita turned the radio back up. She tapped her thumb on the edge of the steering wheel. Right now she felt wide awake. And she felt other things too. Happy to be on the way to New Orleans. Proud of Marco. Lonely for her papa. Itchy to do something with her fingers.

And then out of the blue, she said, "Jacks!" and took her hands off the steering wheel for half a second—no worry of falling asleep—and snapped her fingers.

All of a sudden she had a vision of her *abuelo* playing jacks with her great-uncles in front of his house—she hadn't thought of that since she was a little girl—and she wished her papa were alive. Why hadn't they ever played? It was a family game that he'd liked, but she could have used her hands instead of her feet. It wasn't something Papa had thought was silly, like art.

Margarita would play jacks with Marco, then. In honor of Papa. She'd buy a bag of jacks and a few rubber balls, maybe rainbow-colored balls—*rojo, anaranjado, amarillo, verde, azul, púrpura*—and teach Marco how to play when she got home.

chapter 17

ZAVION

"I think I might have kneaded the bread too much," said Zavion.

Night was hard.

He didn't sleep much, and when he did, he had the same nightmare.

And that made the next morning hard too.

"I don't know what went wrong. I kneaded forty-five times—" He winced as he pulled on the bread. "It's too tough. I'm sorry—"

"No apologies, Zavion, honey," said Ms. Cyn. "It's bread. It's flexible." She chuckled. "It stretches just fine." She pulled on a corner of the dough and let go. It snapped back.

"But it's better to knead less than knead more. I have to remember that—"

"It's all a process, Zavion. You're a good learner."

Zavion did have to admit that even though he could do better, he was getting the hang of this bread-making thing. It was only his second day on the job and he had made the bread by himself. It was his job now. He was putting the two loaves on the paddle when the kitchen door opened and three men—the clowns—tumbled in.

"Do they always travel together?" said Zavion.

"Yes, they seem to," said Ms. Cyn.

"Yup, we do," said Enzo.

"We've all got plenty of biceps—" said Tavius, flexing his arms.

"—but not enough brains," said Skeet.

"A third each," said Tavius. He flicked Skeet and Enzo on their foreheads. "One, two"—he tapped himself—"three."

"Together we have a fighting chance," said Skeet.

"Sometimes I'm not so sure about that," said Ms. Cyn, pouring cups of coffee. "Where were you?"

"The question is—" said Enzo.

"—where are *you*?" said Tavius.

"Or *who* are you?" said Skeet. "My mother-in-law would never set even one tiny baby toe in the kitchen—" Ms. Cyn swatted Skeet with a dish towel. "Just kidding. Sort of. But not really." She spun the towel and swatted him again. "Oooooh-wheeee! All right! We went to Diana's house."

"The bird lady?" said Ms. Cyn.

"Yup. Birds everywhere," said Enzo.

"And a vet is staying at her house too," said Tavius. "She said they've rescued more than one hundred birds already."

"Diana said she gets twenty calls a day from families who had to evacuate and leave their birds behind," said Skeet.

"Why were you visiting Diana?" Ms. Cyn settled herself at the kitchen table and picked up her scarf and knitting needles.

"We wanted to see if we could help," said Tavius.

"Go back into New Orleans with her," said Enzo.

"Maybe catch some birds," said Skeet.

"And ... ," said Ms. Cyn.

"She said we'd just be in the way," said Skeet.

"Us!" said Enzo.

"Can you believe it?" said Tavius.

"Do you want me to even answer that?" Ms. Cyn looked up from her knitting and grinned. Zavion stared at her long trail of orange scarf. "You three clowns in the way?" It was enormous now. He wondered how big the person who was getting the scarf was. Maybe it was for Enzo, Skeet, and Tavius all at once!

"You can never have too much of us!" said Skeet. He reached into the bowl at the center of the table and pulled out three apples. He tossed one to Tavius and one to Enzo. "Right, boys?"

They circled Ms. Cyn and tossed the apples to one another over her head.

"Hey, now—" she protested.

"Hush, Ms. Cyn," said Skeet. "We got it—"

"—together—" said Tavius.

"—oooh, baby, do we ever," finished Enzo. And as if on cue, they all spun in a circle and bit down on their apples at the same time.

Zavion couldn't help smiling.

The clowns bowed. "Thank you, thank you," said Skeet.

"Tip jar is by the door on your way out," said Enzo.

"Don't you let these fools steal your money, Zavion, honey," said Ms. Cyn. She clucked her tongue and shook her head as she bent over her knitting again.

Steal.

The word punctured the corners of Zavion's upturned mouth like a pin.

The chocolate bars bounced around in his head like those apples. He should pay back what he owed Luna Market. He knew where it was.

But how?

Mama's story came to him then. Or his question. The question he asked every time she told him the story. She'd be at the edge of his bed, pulling the blanket to his chin. He'd sit up fast, the blanket falling, his nose an inch away from her nose.

"How?" he'd demand. "How does a mountain travel from one place to another? How is that possible?"

"Zavion, honey—"

Zavion's head snapped up. He opened his eyes. He hadn't even known they were closed. Had he been talking out loud? Enzo, Skeet, and Tavius sat on the counters around the kitchen and Ms. Cyn still sat at the table, her knitting needles *click-clack*ing, her eyes shining again.

"Are you okay?" she said.

I will never be okay, thought Zavion.

"Are you kidding?" said Enzo. "No one in this house is okay."

"Especially you," said Tavius, slapping Enzo on the back.

"Yeah, you never were," said Skeet.

They laughed, and Zavion appreciated the shift of focus.

How would anything ever be okay again?

How could he pay back the market?

He didn't know, but he knew he had to figure it out. If he could just pay back the money for the chocolate bars, maybe he could make this whole hurricane mess go away.

The sound of laughter interrupted Zavion's thoughts. Ms. Cyn's head was thrown back as she laughed, her laughter like bread dough, like a mountain, rising into the air.

chapter 18

HENRY

Henry sat at the top of the driveway and threw a rubber ball for Brae, who raced down the hill chasing it. How could Mom have done that? How could he have let it happen? How could the marble be gone?

Before that night on the mountain, Henry and Wayne had rules for exchanging the marble. They weren't official or anything. They weren't written down and hung up in their bedrooms. But they were rules that they just *knew*, and they seemed to work.

The marble worked.

Henry's football team rarely lost a game, and when they did it was because of Nopie and his stupid butterfingers. Apple pie fingers. And Wayne's soccer and baseball teams never lost. There was something about accepting the marble, and then holding it, feeling its smooth circle go round and round and round that inspired a sense of invincibility in Henry. He didn't even have to think about feeling invincible. It wasn't a thought. It just *was*. It was hope and bravery and confidence all rolled together just like he rolled the marble in his hand.

It was true that he found the marble the day he and Mom moved into their house. After he had picked his room, he found it on the windowsill. And it was also true that he met Wayne that same afternoon. Everyone knew those parts of the story. What they didn't know was the first part. The part about Henry getting up early in the morning, that morning he and Mom moved, and Henry feeling so heavy with sadness that he laid himself down in the driveway in front of the car and wouldn't get up. Not for breakfast, his last scrambled-egg breakfast in the only house he had ever known, not to play in the tree house his father had built, and not even when Mom finally got into the car and turned it on. She had to lift him up kicking and screaming, hold him back against the seat of the car with her elbow while she wrestled with his seat belt. She surprised him with a bag of cheese puffs for the ride, but even his favorite food didn't make him feel better.

Henry remembered believing it was the end of the world. What did he know? He was only four years old. He also re-membered grabbing onto one idea and squeezing it until it was blue. If there was a sign at the new house, then he knew he would live beyond that last day in the old brown house.

So he had walked upstairs, picked his new room, and there it had been. Right on the windowsill.

The marble.

And now it was gone.

The thought made Henry want to lie down again, this time in front of the car or pickup or eighteen-wheeler or whatever had driven off with the marble. He lay down in his driveway instead, beside Brae, who was chewing on the rubber ball.

"What am I going to do?" he asked Brae. Brae leaned in to sniff Henry's nose. "Do you smell an idea?" said Henry, rubbing Brae under the chin. "'Cause I don't feel anything cooking in here—" He tapped the side of his head. Cooking made Henry think of Nopie and his stupid apple pie, and he said, "Stupid!" out loud and then he said, "Oh, not you, Brae! Never you! You're the smartest dog-cow I know—" He sat up, took the ball, put his hands inside his sweatshirt pocket. "Which hand?" he said. Brae sniffed Henry again, this time around his pocket, and nudged Henry's left hand. "Right!" Henry said. "You're right every time!" He threw the ball again and watched Brae as he raced down the driveway.

Suddenly, his brain was racing too.

Suddenly, his brain was an oven and he was cooking up an idea fast.

If Brae could chase a ball, why couldn't Henry chase a marble?

The marble was in New Orleans.

Jake was going to New Orleans.

Henry could hitch a ride with Jake and find his marble.

This was a triple-decker cake of an idea!

Brae loped back up the driveway and dropped the ball at Henry's feet. He licked Henry. "Do I taste sweet, Brae?" said Henry. "Cake sweet?"

And right there at the top of the driveway, under Mount Mansfield, Henry felt the heat of a tiny bit of hope.

"I'll ask Mom if I can go," said Henry. "She'll let me go." He paused. "No, she won't. Shoot." He paused again. The heat-spark flickered dramatically. Hope, no hope, hope, no hope. "What am I going to do, Brae? I need to get that marble. But how? What would Wayne do?" Brae stared into Henry's eyes. "You've got the answer, don't you? What is it?" Henry stood up fast, almost knocking Brae in the nose. "Right! He'd sneak onto the truck! That's what he'd do. And that's what I'm gonna do." He took a deep breath. "Who am I kidding? I can't sneak onto Jake's truck." He looked into Brae's eyes again. "Okay, yeah, you're right. I'm just going to have to talk to Jake. I'm going to have to get Jake to convince Mom that I can go."

With that, Henry turned up the heat on his cake, on his triple-decker, perfect cake of an idea.

CORA KRISHNASWAMI

Marble cake! That was it! She couldn't wait to go to the kitchen in the back of the Salvation Army and bake it.

Cora wanted to try making a marble cake with three flavors swirled together. The usual marble cake was two. Chocolate and vanilla. But that was a little too ordinary for the occasion, Cora thought. *Two* ordinary. Cora laughed at the joke inside her head.

"Pardon?" The woman at the counter looked up from writing her check.

"Hmmmm? Oh, no, nothing—something I just thought of—" Cora unclipped her hair and let it fall across her shoulders.

Like toilet paper tucked in the waistband of a pair of blue jeans, Cora always managed to drag embarrassing stuff out into the public. She couldn't seem to keep the roll of thoughts she had from spilling out of her mouth.

"Sorry," she said. "I didn't even know I laughed out loud."

This time it wasn't so bad. Just a random laugh. But people were sensitive these days. Cora knew that. They'd been through so much—too much—and there was nothing funny about any of it. She was lucky. Her small house had been spared. But not her neighbor's. His house sat lower than hers and it got flooded even when hers did not.

"Well, it's important to find something to laugh about," said the woman. She picked up her shopping bag from the counter.

"Yes," agreed Cora. The woman was generous. She could have been put off by Cora's laugh. Her neighbor could have been put off by her too. If he had been able to hear her over the rain and wind. Of course she had blurted out that she was *queen of the mountain* as she stood on her front porch as the rain and wind came down. She still didn't know why she had said that. She had stepped outside for just a moment and was overcome by the raging battle taking place all around her little house. Knives of rain clattering down. The shriek of the wind. And she was, on her covered porch, just above it all. She had felt a sense of relief, and a weird thrill, and before she knew it, this *queen* thing had escaped from her mouth.

Just half a second later, she turned her head and saw her neighbor on his roof, water pouring out of his downstairs front window. Cora had seen him on the roof plenty of times before—he hung out up there with his daughter sometimes, but mostly with two other men. His brothers. They came over to her neighbor's house and sang up there a lot, and she loved to listen to them.

"Do you have any children?" Cora asked the woman.

"Yes," said the woman. "Why?"

"We just got a big donation from Vermont," said Cora. "I haven't gone through all of it, but there are some great kids' clothes." She indicated a pile on the side counter. "Take a look. Someone is about to come by and take them to Baton Rouge."

The woman walked to the clothes and thumbed through a stack. She pulled a pair of blue jeans from the middle and unfolded them. "These look almost new," she said.

Cora nodded.

"But they're too long for my son." She began to fold them again.

"Oh, I'll do that," said Cora. She took the jeans from the woman.

"I should get home to him," said the woman. "I'm starting to let him stay home alone, but only for an hour or so at a time."

"How old is he?" asked Cora.

"Ten," said the woman.

"Sort of an in-between age, huh? A little too young to stay home alone, but also a little too old to need supervision?" asked Cora.

"Yes, exactly." The woman began to walk toward the door. "I'll be back," she said. "I'm so glad you're open."

"What do you think of chocolate, peanut butter, cinnamon cake?" Cora blurted out.

"It sounds delicious," said the woman.

"Oh good. To me too," said Cora. "Three cheers for the generator! I'm trying to make a marble cake with three flavors. Three cheers for three flavors!"

"Sounds complicated."

"It's for three things, so I thought three flavors would be a nice touch."

The woman smiled.

"Thing One: I hope that you—oh, not you"—Cora pointed at the woman—"you, my neighbor, move back home. Thing Two: I love listening to you and your trio sing. And Thing Three: I'm sorry for what I said out there in the hurricane—" The words tumbled out of Cora's mouth.

The woman stared at her.

Cora shook her head. She had gone and done it again. Toilet paper in the waist of the jeans, right there in public. She twisted her hair back into a bun and clipped it into place. She could at least keep her hair neat.

She looked down at the blue jeans in her hands and slowly finished folding them. By the time she looked up, maybe the woman would be gone.

chapter 19

ZAVION

Zavion knew it was wishful thinking, thinking if he could just pay back the money for the chocolate bars he could make the whole hurricane mess go away. But he still felt like he had to try.

Zavion found Papa in the living room hunched over a tiny canvas.

A tiny square slate roof shingle, actually.

The kind Zavion had given as an IOU at Luna Market. More shingles were scattered all over the table.

Zavion had overheard Tavius and Enzo offering them to Skeet and Papa.

"We figured Skeet could use them for some art project, so we collected them as we walked," said Tavius.

"You should have seen us. Waterlogged and weighed down with these shingles in our pockets," said Enzo.

"It gave us something to focus on," said Tavius.

"You should use them too," said Enzo to Papa. "Make lemonade out of lemons."

"Make slate-ade out of slate," said Tavius.

Zavion had watched as Papa picked up a piece of slate and turned it slowly in his hands.

Now he was painting on one.

"What's up, Zav?"

Zavion knew for a fact that if mothers had eyes in the back of their heads, fathers had them on top of theirs. How many times had Papa been bent over a mural sketch working but still knew that he had entered the room?

It wasn't Mama's soft-eyed stare and bear-hug combination, but it was still comforting. Most of the time. Not today, though. But that wasn't Papa's fault. Zavion was on a specific, scary mission today.

Zavion sat down across from Papa. His short hair was grayer than Zavion could remember seeing before. Papa's hair was often all different colors—he had a habit of rubbing his fingers into his scalp while he was painting—but this gray was not paint.

Zavion breathed in the familiar smell of acrylic mixed with hair relaxer and cedar deodorant. It was the only familiar thing his body had experienced since they left their house to slog through the water, and it made him suddenly and forcefully sad.

"What are you painting, Papa?" he asked.

He was stalling for time before he asked his question. The question that could only have one answer.

"Tiny landscapes."

"You never paint tiny."

"True."

"You've only ever painted one landscape."

"True too."

Papa's paintings were of Mardi Gras and musicians and fishing for shrimp and oysters and catfish. They were huge too. He usually painted right across a whole wall.

"Sometimes the world tells you to do something new." Hearing that made Zavion's sadness break apart like fireworks. Maybe this wouldn't be so hard. Maybe Papa was ready for something different. "I woke up with this mighty strong urge to paint some very small landscapes," continued Papa. He picked up a slate shingle that was drying next to him. "The slate makes the colors pop," he said. "And it feels good to hold this tree in my hands." He opened his fingers so the shingle balanced in the middle of his palm. "It's in one piece. I can see the whole thing."

The tree was from the Appalachian spruce-fir forest.

"A red spruce?" Zavion asked, but he was sure he was right. Its green needle-tipped branches reached to the very edges of the shingle, and the sky around it was a tropical blue, almost like the sea, but quieter and flat, no brushstrokes to indicate waves. "Mama's tree?"

Papa nodded.

It was the tree at the top of the mural that Papa had painted in Zavion's room. The tree that stood on top of Grand-mother Mountain, where Mama had grown up. It wasn't actually there—the University of North Carolina Public Tele-vision broadcasting tower was on top of the real Grandmother Mountain—but Papa had given Mama a red spruce on theirs.

Zavion wanted to climb the tree, jump from the ground to its lowest branch and climb all the way to the top, all the way to the still, silent sky.

"I like it," he said.

He had to do it.

He had to ask Papa now.

"Speaking of the world telling you to do something new—" he began.

"Yes?" said Papa, placing the red spruce tree down again and picking up his paintbrush.

Zavion picked up his own dry paintbrush and pushed it along the wooden table, tracing the shape of a mountain, as if a picture would speak to Papa better than words.

"We need to go to Mama's mountain."

"We've had this discussion."

That didn't sound like a promising beginning. Maybe a picture really would be better. Zavion was going to have to be clearer.

"No, we haven't had a discussion about this. We've had a mention of it."

"A mention?"

"Yes, I mentioned it and you made fun of me, and then you left the kitchen."

Papa dipped his paintbrush in water and wiped it dry with a rag. He squeezed a dot of orange paint onto the corner of the slate. "Why don't you go for a run, Zavion? Wouldn't that feel good?"

Zavion couldn't imagine running. He was exhausted. Trying not to think about . . . before . . . was exhausting.

"Let's go to Mama's mountain," he tried again.

"I don't know why you are so obsessed with this mountain idea."

Zavion stuck his paintbrush in the orange paint on Papa's slate and grabbed a slate of his own. "Ask me." He painted the top.

Papa opened the pink paint and squeezed it next to the orange. "Why do you want to go to that mountain, then?"

Zavion dipped his paintbrush in the pink and added it to the edge of the orange. He unscrewed the red paint and stuck the tip of his paintbrush in the top. He blurred it into the edge of the pink. He tried to remember the shape of the mural in his room and drew the jagged edge of a mountain and filled around it with red paint.

Before came flooding in.

Except for Papa, everything he had known his whole life was gone. The big oak tree and its shade and the brick walkway leading up to his house. Gone. The house. Gone. Everything inside the house. Gone. And the one last thing that had reminded him of Mama. Gone.

All of them swept away in the hurricane.

And before that—Mama herself. She was gone too.

After Mama died, Zavion spent every waking moment searching for a way to feel like he wouldn't just float away. And after the moments turned to days, and the days turned to weeks, and the weeks to months—seven months, to be exact—he had found it. It was in the pathway from the bathroom through the art studio across the hall and into his bedroom, the long way to his room after he brushed his teeth, but he walked it the same way each night. It was on the slices of bread he laid out every morning, between the peanut butter and the honey, tucked tight into the wax paper bag he placed in the backpack he took to school. It was tied in the laces of his lucky running sneakers. It was on the thin rim of the molding over the archway between the kitchen and the living room he jumped to touch every time he passed through. And it was embedded in the gray rocks that sat across the edge of his windowsill, each of them with a white crystal line running through the middle—rocks he had found by the river, made wishes on, and placed on his sill to come true—all these routines and rituals designed and practiced and perfected in order to feel like his feet were firmly on the ground.

And always, always, Grandmother Mountain standing guard over Zavion as he slept each night and woke each morning to begin his maze of a day once again.

That mountain—Mama's mountain—

And now everything from his room, his home, his life, was—

    maybe—

        maybe not—

          probably—

            surely—

              completely—

                gone.

Zavion put down his paintbrush and held the white mountain—rising up inside the blazing sunset—in his hand.

"Because sometimes the world tells you to do something new," he said.

chapter 20

HENRY

"Please, Jake."

Henry watched Jake close the door to the trailer on the eighteen-wheeler. He was doing a last check of the truck before he headed out of town.

"Please let me come with you."

"I don't know, Henry." He opened the driver's side door of the cab and climbed in. He turned the headlights on, then turned them off. He turned the windshield wipers on, then turned them off.

Henry put his hand on the giant cab door and looked up at Jake.

"I need to get out of here," he said.

Jake started the truck. It rumbled to life. Henry felt its vibration through the metal. A buzzing feeling in his hand.

"Jake—" he said.

Jake was testing the gears.

"Jake—" he said louder.

Nothing.

"*Jake!*" he yelled above the engine roar.

Jake turned his head. He cut the engine. Henry's heart was racing from raising his voice. "I need—" Henry began. But he didn't know what to say. He looked past Jake, out through the passenger window to Mount Mansfield. "I want—" he tried again.

Jake jumped down from the cab. He began inspecting the front tire, running his hand along its tread.

"The red-breasted goose in the Siberian tundra is vulnerable to arctic fox attacks," Henry said all of a sudden. "The foxes are always hungry. They'll eat the geese in an instant. If the geese build their nests alone, the foxes eat their eggs and chicks too. Like that—" Henry snapped his fingers. "But they don't make their nests alone. They wait until the peregrine falcons build *their* nests, and then the geese build theirs around them. The peregrine falcons fight off the arctic fox." Henry paused.

Jake stared at him, listening intently.

"The peregrine falcon is small but fierce," finished Henry.

"National Geographic special?"

"PBS."

"Cool birds. I can always count on you to find the cool animals."

Henry looked Jake right in the eyes. "I want to be a peregrine falcon, Jake." He glanced out the cab window again. The edges of Mount Mansfield glimmered under the sun. He looked back at Jake. "I can help in New Orleans."

Jake leaned against the truck. He stuffed his hands in his pockets.

"It isn't going to be easy there."

"I know."

"It isn't going to be pretty."

"I know."

"Have you seen it on TV? It's ... pure survival," said Jake. "Nothing pretty about it."

"Nothing pretty about here," said Henry, glancing back at the stupid hulking mountain one more time.

Jake nodded slowly. He pressed his lips together and took in a deep breath through his nose. "Nope," he finally said. "You're right about that." He turned and looked at Henry. "I gotta go. I can't explain it, but I need to be in the middle of that city. I need to be right there in the middle of that hurricane-torn place, like maybe it will stop my own spinning—" He laughed. It was a sad, small sound. "I'm a nut, is all."

"You're a peregrine falcon," said Henry. "Me too." He held his breath, the air inside him filled with hope.

"Okay, bird boy," said Jake. "I'll take you with me. If your mother says it's okay."

Henry blew the air out of his body. And the hope that he had held spun and curled into the wind and headed south, which happened to be the way the wind was traveling.

chapter 21
ZAVION

Zavion had to get to Grandmother Mountain. That one thought was crystal clear in his mind. As crystal clear as the white lines running through the middle of his wishing rocks.

Somewhere there was a person who could take him there.

But before that, Zavion had a debt to pay. He had to find a way to get money. He had to find a way to get Papa to take him back to New Orleans. He had to slow down his heart.

PIERRE DUCHAMP

Pierre opened the bag of clothes from the New Orleans Salvation Army.

Shirts.

Socks.

Boxer shorts.

Sweatshirts.

A pair of blue jeans.

He knew the people who came in to his Salvation Army. The Baton Rouge branch. He thought of them as *his* people.

They were certainly more his people than his own family.

His own family opened their arms wide in the middle of winter, heads thrown back to the sky, mouths open, drinking in the wet, cold snowflakes. The more snow the better. They worshipped it. His brother snowboarded. His sister skied. His sister's son played ice hockey, and her daughter did too. She was only ten, but she was already on a team. Had even won a few medals.

And his mother—well, his mother stayed home and made the hot chocolate. She couldn't watch any of them. Couldn't stand to watch the speed. Downhill, across the ice, or falling fast from the sky. Ever since her husband, Pierre's father, had been killed in an avalanche back-country skiing. She couldn't bear it that all her children had been born with their father's deep devotion to the snow and speed. She worried for them just as she had worried for her husband.

But she was also proud. She saw her husband in each of them.

Except for Pierre. Because Pierre hated the snow. Even before it took his father away, he'd hated it. Hated how it melted into his skin and numbed him on the inside. And after his father was killed, he hated how it reminded him of his father.

So he had left the snow behind, left his family, and moved down to Louisiana.

He loved the thick, warm air here.

He loved the thick accents and the warm people.

He felt at home.

Even during Hurricane Katrina he had loved the city. In

fact, he had found his bravery in that very storm. Saved a little girl who had been sucked into the water and carried away from her house.

Calm-bodied and clearheaded, he had stayed in the rising river for a good part of that first night, helping to rescue people.

The bell rang above the front door of the store.

"Hey, Tavius," said Pierre.

"Hey there, Pierre. How are you?" said Tavius.

"Happy to see you," he said—and then he blushed. "I heard a few more folks have come to live with your brother," he added quickly.

"Yup."

"A boy and his father?"

"You have some magical antennae, don't you? I was just saying to Enzo, that you're like a butterfly—"

Pierre blushed a second time.

"Don't they—don't butterflies—they have an ability to smell with—you know—with their antennae?" said Tavius. "Not that you really have antennae . . ." He trailed off as he put two fingers on either side of his head. He wiggled them and laughed. Pierre laughed too.

"The butterflies are at the peak of their life cycles this time of year," said Pierre.

"They sure are," said Tavius. There was a pause.

Pierre put his fingers up to his head too, and wiggled them. "I like being a butterfly," he said. "Peak of my life cycle. I like that."

Tavius beamed.

"Here," said Pierre, taking his antennae down and picking up the garbage bag. "Take this bag of clothes. It just came from Cora in New Orleans. There's some good stuff in here. I'm betting the boy who just came to live with you could use it."

Tavius reached for the bag. His hand grazed Pierre's as he took hold of it. Pierre looked up at him and smiled. Tavius was *his* people, that was for sure. Maybe even his one person.

"Hey," he said. "Before you go home. Do you want to get some coffee? Or go for a walk?"

chapter 22

HENRY

Mom had needed a little coaxing to give her blessing.

"You really want to go, Henry?" she asked. She sat on the front steps, dirt smeared across the knees of her blue jeans.

Henry nodded. He was perched on top of the fence at the side of the house. Jake leaned against it next to him.

"I don't know—"

"Please, Mom—"

"It's just so far away.... How safe is it? What if it's too hard to be there ... in the middle of all that ... chaos? Jake has a job to do. He can't just turn around and come home if you decide you want to leave—" Mom ran her hands through her hair and left a mark of dirt on her forehead.

"It might be good for him, Eliza," said Jake. His voice was quiet. "I can tell you I'm counting on that for me."

Henry watched Mom look at Jake. She bit her lip.

"You told me I didn't need to go to school right now, re-member?" said Henry.

"I remember. But what about seeing your dad on Monday?"

"Mom, I can miss that, can't I?"

Mom nodded. "You really don't mind taking him, Jake?"

"I promised him a trip. I'd better make good on it." Jake smiled, but it stopped at his cheeks. His eyes looked sad.

Mom stood up then. She walked over to Henry and put her hands on his knees. Her fingernails were caked in dirt too.

"You go, then," she said. "Okay?"

"Okay," said Henry.

"Help Jake, okay?"

"Okay."

Mom looked at Jake. "I guess he's yours," she said. She touched Jake's shoulder. "Thank you." Then she sighed. "I'll miss you, Henry. And who's going to help me in the garden?"

"Brae will—"

At the sound of his name, Brae dropped the stick he was chewing and tipped his head to the side.

Saying good-bye to Mom had been hard, but saying it to Brae was harder.

Brae had put his head into Henry's lap as soon as Henry sat

up in bed the next morning. Henry scratched him behind the ears. "I'm gonna miss you, boy," he said. After he'd put on his football jersey, he asked Brae to sit, lifted his chin, and looked straight into his eyes. "Don't learn any new tricks while I'm gone, okay?"

Brae licked his nose.

Henry's ears were vibrating with scraps of sound. Boxes being dragged, boots shuffling, the three-note tune Jake endlessly whistled. Henry craned his neck from his seat in the front of the truck and saw a group of big-rig drivers by the police station, drinking cups of coffee. There was Jake, talking to the one woman there.

Stacks of bags and boxes were piled high in the back of the trailer. What was in them? Maybe Little League shirts or yo-yos or comic books or cookies. What would a kid all the way down in New Orleans do with a Green Mountain Insurance Company baseball shirt? One of the bags looked like it was full of stuffed animals, a black and white cow peeked its head out the top. Were there cows in Louisiana? Henry thought of the kinds of animals that were in New Orleans. He'd looked them up. Alligators, feral pigs, yellow warblers, shorebirds. And lots of butterflies this time of year. He'd also looked up how far Louisiana was from Vermont. Almost sixteen hundred miles.

Henry thought about how many times a marble would have to turn to get from here to there. He shook his head. Wayne would know how to do the math to figure that one out. Henry didn't have a freaking clue.

How long had it taken his marble to get to New Orleans? It hadn't rolled there—that was for sure. It had traveled just like he was about to, tucked away in a truck. Henry couldn't believe it. Here he was, in the parking lot of the state police department, in Jake's truck, almost on his way to New Orleans. He and Wayne had always wanted to go on a road trip with Jake. And Jake had promised them—this year would be their year—

And now—

Now—

Wayne couldn't go. He would never be able to go.

Across the parking lot, a trucker Henry didn't recognize put a box into his trailer. The clouds behind him moved as he moved, like he was loading them onto the truck too, like he was shipping Vermont skies south with the yo-yos and comic books and cookies.

Jake climbed into his seat. "This is going to be quite a field trip," he said. "I was talking with one of the other truckers—not a regular—her name is Margarita—do you know her? She lives in Underhill too, just moved there last year. She teaches Spanish, actually—I should tell Annie— Anyway, Margarita just got back. She said that the smell of garbage in New Orleans is overwhelming. The food-and-clothing drive coordinator said the same thing, and Margarita confirmed it. Cat litter and rotting milk, she said. Are you sure you're prepared for all that?"

Henry was never prepared for a math test, no matter how many practice problems his teacher gave.

He was never prepared for how lonely he felt at his dad's house, even though he had gone there every Monday for the last six years of his life and his dad had a houseful of kids.

No, he was not prepared.

Jake laughed. "Me neither," he said before Henry had even opened his mouth. "Being prepared is not the issue. The issue is what you do when you're taken by surprise."

"Here—" said a voice.

Who was that? Henry leaned around Jake to look down at the ground. Talk about a surprise—a bad surprise! Nopie! Nopie was talking to Jake. "Some apple pie. I thought you could eat it on the ride."

"That was mighty thoughtful of you," said Jake. "Thank you. And thank your mom for me, okay?"

"Okay," said Nopie. "Good luck down there."

"Thanks."

Nopie stared up at Jake with his crazy-wide turtle eyes. *Jeez.* Wasn't he going to leave?

"Aren't you going to wish me good luck too?" said Nopie finally.

"Good luck?" asked Jake.

"For finding Tiger."

Oh man! Give it up, Nopie. Didn't he know he wasn't going to find him?

There was another, smaller pause, and then Jake said quietly, "Good luck, then, Nopie."

And then Jake slammed the door shut and started up the truck.

He turned onto the highway and opened the window. A thin sliver of wind found its way through the crack and blew across Henry's face, and he felt freer and freer as they moved farther and farther away from the mountain.

TAVIUS TATE

In the end, Tavius and Pierre had gone for coffee *and* a walk. And then for pie and another walk, and finally they ended up back at the Salvation Army, where they sat on the front steps and talked for the rest of the night.

Tavius put his fingers on the sides of his head and wiggled them like anntenae reaching for the early-morning light. The sun warmed his face and matched the cozy feeling that grew the more he talked with Pierre. He grinned and snapped his fingers, still up high in the air. He was excited.

Truth be told, Tavius was excited to be staying at Skeet's house too. Of course he wasn't happy that Hurricane Katrina had descended upon them all, knocking them upside their heads and back down their backsides. But, as he slung the bag of clothes over his shoulder, whistling as he walked the eleven blocks back to Skeet's house, he had to admit that he liked living with his brothers again.

He saw them plenty. It wasn't about not seeing them. He and Skeet went to Enzo's once a week after work for a cold glass of something sweet, to shoot the breeze and sing a few songs up on the roof. He looked forward to that.

But this was better. Lots more chances for laughing. There was nothing better in the whole wide world than a joke catching the funny bone by surprise. Enzo and Skeet were full of the kind that sent Tavius into snorting, wheezing, knee-slapping fits of laughter.

He loved living with Enzo's sharp-as-a-tack kid, Osprey. That was the truest truth to tell. And Ms. Cyn, who reminded him of his mama, he loved her too. And truth be told one more ever-loving time—he was growing fond of Ben and Zavion too.

Just the night before, the seven of them had sat in the kitchen after supper, drinking sweet tea and eating the last bits of Zavion's bread until they all thought they would burst. Then Osprey turned off the lights and said—

Lady and Gentlemen, I will now perform a song for your enjoyment—

Seriously, where did the kid get this stuff?

But first, a public service announcement for the lady: rest assured, there are no creepy snakes in this kitchen—

Which began the laughter, and then Osprey proceeded to sing her rendition of "When the Saints Go Marching In," only she sang *sanes* instead of *saints*, which made a whole lot more sense and which set off a whole other round of laughter. Even Zavion smiled the littlest bit, which warmed up Tavius's heart in a way he couldn't explain.

Now he knew he couldn't wait to catch Zavion coming out of the bathroom, or in the front door, or working in the kitchen, unawares, and make some joke about the word *sane* and have the chance to see that small smile again.

Shared jokes like that were the two-by-fours that kept a house standing tall. They were logs on the fire and a good smell curling out of the oven. They were what Tavius remembered from being a kid with two older brothers and a mother whose laugh he could hear down the block as he walked home from school. They were what had been missing from his house in New Orleans.

They were what held Skeet's house together now.

Even after Katrina knocked them upside their heads.

And on the top of it all, he had gotten to meet Pierre.

Tavius whistled louder.

He couldn't wait to give Zavion the new clothes.

chapter 23

ZAVION

Something hard was in the pocket of Zavion's new blue jeans.

He stuck his hand inside.

A marble.

A big marble.

Blue like the sky when there's no rain. Green too, like a mountain. And some red and orange. Like fire? Flashes of light?

Zavion had other questions. One, really.

Whose marble was it?

Then another question followed.

Where did it come from?

And the question that bit hard on the heels of the others.

Did Zavion have to give it back?

Zavion was used to finding the answers outside of himself like on his Spanish pop quiz, where one side of the paper had numbered Spanish words and the other side had lettered English words.

1. *El perro*   goes with   E. Dog
2. *El gato*   goes with   L. Cat
3. *El pájaro*   goes with   O. Bird

But he didn't have answers to his questions now.

The marble felt smooth against the inside of Zavion's fingers. It felt good to wrap his hand around something whole. It made him feel big. Like he could sweep his other hand across the sky and gather the hurricane up tight, gather all that wind and rain, close his fist hard around it, and blow the dust away.

The desire for this hurricane-crushing ability surprised Zavion. It pounded over the memories that had taken permanent residence inside him. Snakes. Oily water. A dead body.

The marble made him feel like he could jump back into New Orleans, jump with his knees bent and his thigh muscles gripping—like he was doing the standing long jump—and land with both feet hard, right into the middle of his street, right next to where his house used to be, with a huge splash that would send the three-feet-deep water into the sky, miles high and miles wide.

Zavion held the marble up to his eye. He could just make out Papa in the dining room, hunched over another tiny canvas. A blue, green, red, and orange Papa. Like a painting of Papa. A painting of Papa painting.

That struck Zavion as funny and so he laughed. Which felt strange. He hadn't laughed in a long time. And something about laughing made him feel . . . hopeful.

The door blew open and Osprey ran in. "Zavion!" She flung her cold hands around Zavion's neck. "What do you have in your hand?" she said.

She didn't miss anything.

"What do you have in yours?" said Zavion. A leash dangled behind her with a washcloth tied to one end.

"This"—Osprey pulled the leash close to her side—"is Fluffer." She reached down and patted the washcloth.

"Where's Flower?"

"She ran away. Now, show me what's in your hand!"

"Nothing's there," said Zavion, slipping the marble back into his pocket.

"Do you have a secret?" said Osprey.

"Well, I wouldn't tell you if I did, right?"

"Would you tell Fluffer?"

"Not even Fluffer."

Osprey stood on her tiptoes and grabbed Zavion around

the neck. She leaned in close to his ear. "Do you have a magic?" she whispered.

A magic. Zavion liked that.

It sounded like his wishing rocks with their white stripes lined up on his windowsill.

Yes!

The marble was just like his wishing rocks.

He squeezed it in his hand and smiled. He could feel the bright blue, green, red, and orange radiating their colors against his palm. Like the moon on the river. Or the sunset over a marsh.

Like a magic.

"Yes," said Zavion, still smiling. "I have a magic."

And if the marble was a magic, then wasn't the person who put it in the pocket of the jeans a magician? And didn't magicians make things appear just where they wanted them to?

That meant the marble was supposed to come to him.

Didn't it?

chapter 24
HENRY

Jake adjusted the rearview mirror. The carabiner clipped
around the mirror swung and the silver baseball flashed bright
in the sun.

"I knew you weren't sleeping at your house. I knew you
were up on the mountain that night," said Jake. "I used to sleep
up there too."

"You did?"

Jake adjusted the mirror again. He hit the baseball with
the back of his hand, and it swung so hard it flipped over the
carabiner, shortening its chain. "Yup. I snuck out of the house
on a few clear nights when I was about your age."

"You did." This time it wasn't a question.

"Yup. Nothing like the top of Mansfield at night. Feels like
driving to the end of a dead-end road. You're there. That's it.
End of story."

Henry wanted to reach up and stop the baseball from flickering. It made him dizzy. He didn't know what Jake was talking about and he did know, all at the same time, and that made him dizzy too.

"Nothing else there when you're up so high and it's so dark. Just the wind and the moon and the stars. Yup, it sure feels like the end of the road." Jake ran his hand through his hair and put it back on the steering wheel. "Or the beginning, I guess."

Henry stared ahead at the highway. It was straight and flat and stretched on forever, it seemed.

Jake took a deep breath and said very quickly, "Is there anything else you can tell me? About Wayne's accident?"

Henry rolled down the window a little more. The guardrail whizzed by in a gray blur. He opened his mouth and let the wind fill it, and fill his nose and eyes and ears too. It tasted salty and bitter.

What could he tell Jake?

Lying on his belly, at the edge of the cliff, Henry felt and saw little things first. Soft moss under his bare arms. A sapling growing out of a crack in the rock, its roots firmly dug into that small space of dirt. Henry hadn't noticed either of these things when he was flying down the mountain determined to win the race. But he noticed them now, he noticed them first, his mind racing with the fear of what had happened to Wayne. Maybe Wayne had slipped on the moss. Maybe he had grabbed for the tree. Henry imagined Wayne's fall, off the rock, down onto the sloping ledge fifteen feet below, straight into the crevasse—

For the second time that morning, Brae sat on his haunches and threw his head up high and keened to the sky. The sound echoed off the rocks. This time it sounded like Brae was calling— not to the sun and not to the moon—but in the other direction, into the very center of the mountain, into the very center of the earth. The sound of his voice spiraled around the rocks, traveled in a circle down, down, down until it penetrated the earth below Henry's horizontal body—

Waaaaaaaaaaaaaaayne!!!

Henry wanted to keen his name too, send his voice down, down, down to where he knew Wayne lay—

No.

No no no no no no no.

He could not tell Jake what he saw when he finally, finally looked over the edge.

Jake breathed in and it sounded funny, like the air got caught on something in the back of his throat. It was a ragged, shuddery kind of a sound. "Or how about telling me something

Wayne said?" Jake's voice was searching for something, opening cupboards and pulling out drawers.

And there it was.

Something Wayne said.

A shady, hidden memory of the night before the accident—

Henry and Wayne barely needed their headlamps as they hiked up the mountain, the moon was so full and bright. The trees were shorter up this high, more like shrubs than trees, and the sound of rustling branches came at their knees instead of above their heads. It was a softer sound too, the branches were covered with needles not leaves. Soon they used their hands to climb up steep rock faces. Brae bounded ahead of them, leaping on and off the rocks three times for every one grab their fingers made.

Then they were at the top.

"We made it!" shouted Wayne, throwing his backpack off his shoulders. He spun in a circle. Brae ran around him.

"Uh, yeah," said Henry. "Like always."

"Never at night, though, Henry. Isn't it amazing up here? Look at the sky. Look at the moon." Wayne continued to spin. He looked like the top of a helicopter, his arms spread wide. Like a helicopter just beginning its flight—

* * *

Henry couldn't bear to remember it. But it was coming. *Oh man, oh man, oh man*, it was coming. He felt sick. He thought he might have to ask Jake to pull over.

Jake looked over his left shoulder and changed lanes. Henry peered into the window of a station wagon as Jake accelerated past it. Two boys were playing cards in the backseat.

"The night before—" Henry took a deep breath. "The night before, when we were on the top of the mountain, we were . . . ummmmm . . . we were talking. A lot. We were talking a lot." They had been too. Henry didn't usually talk that much, he was the nodder or the head shaker. And Wayne was the fists-clenched puncher. But that night they had talked a lot.

Jake switched back into the right lane.

"We . . . ummmmm . . . we talked about—" Henry struggled to say something. To say anything. "How it felt good to be on the mountain," he said miserably. "Wayne said he felt—he said—he loved climbing to the top of the mountain at night."

Was that enough? He did want to give Jake something.

The station wagon sped past the truck. Henry saw the backs of the two boys' heads. They were close together and moving in a jerking motion, back and forth. Henry imagined they were trying to pull cards out of each other's hands.

Jake cleared his throat. "So he was happy?"

Henry nodded.

At that point he had been, anyway.

Jake and Henry drove in silence after that. Henry's brain felt scorched. Like the wind had burnt the clouds that filled his head, and now the sun was too bright and too hot. He didn't want to remember so much. He wanted those clouds back.

The clouds outside turned cream-colored, then yellow, and then a sort of orange. Like the sun had baked them longer and longer as they drove south. The air was thicker too, even saltier, though Henry couldn't believe that was actually possible. Henry saw a dead dog by the side of the highway. He thought he saw its tag gleaming in the sun, and he wanted to stop, but Jake said no. The dog made Henry miss Brae. Crap, he missed him. He missed him in a way that felt like he had been hit in the chest with a baseball so hard it broke through his skin, snapped his ribs, and tore apart his heart.

"I wonder if those two boys in the station wagon ever stopped fighting," he said at one point.

"Don't know" was all Jake said back.

chapter 25

ZAVION

"No, Zavion," said Papa, from his chair in the dining room where he was still painting little landscapes. "No, no, no."

"But Papa—"

"And no."

He was so calm when he argued. No yelling, no sweating, no jumping up from his chair.

"I have to repay the store." Zavion rubbed the marble against his palm with his fingers. It was warm, tucked in his new jeans pocket. Zavion could only hold what fit in his hands now. The marble and chocolate bars.

"I can say it again, if you really want—"

Zavion did *not* want.

"No."

Clearly, it didn't matter what Zavion wanted. It didn't matter what he knew—*he knew*—was the right thing to do. Zavion felt a renewed sense of hope with the magic marble in his pocket. He had already wished on it. Just like he'd done with the wishing rocks. He'd even found a windowsill to sleep near, and he placed the marble there. Just where his wishing rocks had sat. He was hoping it would make him sleep better.

"Let me call the market," said Zavion.

"We don't even know its name. We can't just look up 'market with broken window near the convention center,'" said Papa.

"Luna Market," said Zavion. How did Papa not know that? "On Chartres Street." Until that moment, he hadn't realized that he knew the street name too.

His brain had been functioning that day whether he had known it or not.

"Please, Papa," said Zavion. "Can we try to call?"

Papa put down his paintbrush. "You are bullheaded, boy, do you know that? The phone line at the market is probably down."

"Probably."

"Most likely."

"Maybe, but maybe not," said Zavion.

Papa smiled. "Bullheaded. Just like your Mama." He indicated over his shoulder to a desk with a computer on it. "Use that. See if you can find the number. Then you can call." He pulled a cell phone from his shirt pocket. "I borrowed Skeet's phone to call Gabe. I left him a message."

Zavion walked over to the desk. The computer screen had a map up. He looked at it closely. Point A was Baton Rouge. Point B was Topeka, Kansas.

Zavion needed to act fast.

He typed *Yellow Pages* into the search box and then typed *Luna Market, 311 Chartres Street, New Orleans, Louisiana.*

It was there!

"I found it," said Zavion.

"Here's the phone," said Papa.

Zavion stood behind him and punched in the number. He squeezed the marble with his other hand. For luck. He swallowed hard. What would he say? He hadn't thought about that.

He glanced over Papa's shoulder. The sunlight, streaming in from the side window, lit up a corner of his painting. A purplish-blue color shimmered there. Zavion leaned forward to get a better look. A tiny marsh under a full moon.

Papa seemed obsessed with these landscapes he could hold in his hand. There was something reassuring to Zavion about that.

"Well—" said Papa, startling Zavion.

The phone! Zavion had forgotten that he was on the phone. No ringing. No sound. Silence.

"Nothing," he had to admit. He handed the phone back to Papa.

"Phone lines have to be down," said Papa. He squeezed his eyes shut and opened them again. "It's too soon."

And the way he said it made Zavion think that he meant it was too soon to even think about New Orleans.

"Go on, Zav," said Papa. "You need to go for a run—"

"I need to repay the store," said Zavion.

Papa sighed. "How about you send money later when we get some?"

Zavion couldn't wait until later. He didn't trust that the mail service would get the money to the market. He couldn't risk that. This was something he had to do in person. He had to look the cashier in the eyes. He had to make sure he was understood.

"Please, Papa." He was going to try one more time. "Please take me to New Orleans."

"No."

Zavion knew he would say no.

If Papa wouldn't do it with him, then he was going to do it alone.

"Then I'm going to go by myself." There. He had said it out loud. He felt his heart beating in the wrong place, up against the bottom of his throat.

Papa looked up from his painting. He stared at Zavion without blinking. Zavion had the same wide, long eyelashes—he had Papa's eyes and cheeks, but he had Mama's nose and mouth—and his eyelashes fluttered furiously as he blinked and blinked and blinked while Papa's sat frozen above his eyes.

Zavion knew that Papa usually, eventually, let him do things his way. Even if Papa had more control over his eye muscles and knew how to hold a paintbrush for hours at a time, Zavion was the one who controlled everything else.

Or he used to.

"It's the right thing to do, Papa. So I'm going to do it," he said.

"You will not go back into New Orleans," said Papa slowly.

"But—"

"Do. You. Understand. Me?" Papa spoke even more slowly.

Zavion willed his eyes to stop blinking. He widened them and kept them still even as they dried and he had to fight the urge to blink.

"Why?" He spoke the one word as slowly as he could.

"Because—" Papa looked down then. He closed his eyes. He put down his paintbrush and flexed his fingers and closed them into a fist. He opened his eyes again and opened his fist and shook his hand back and forth. "Because," he finally said again, "I don't want you . . . I can't have you . . . back in that . . .

drowned ... monster of a city ..." He gripped his hands together, interlocking his fingers, and leaned forward. "That ... place ... isn't ... safe...."

Zavion knew about safe. He had made it his job to keep Papa and his own self safe for all these years.

He bent his head down to the floor and finally blinked his eyes. They were wet, but he wasn't crying. He had messed up something *huge* during the hurricane. He rolled the marble from one finger to another in his pocket. It sounded kind of silly, but he believed he had a touch of magic, now that he had found this marble.

He would find some money.

He would find a way to get to New Orleans.

He would find Luna Market.

chapter 26
HENRY

"This bird has a pouch like a kangaroo."

"What is a pelican?"

"This is the largest raptor in the world."

"What is the Andean condor?"

A game show was on the radio.

"Henry ..." Mom's sigh traveled through the telephone like a gust of wind. It blew into Henry's ear and rattled its way to his knees. "Are you all right? Are you eating enough?"

"I just left! How could I not be eating enough?"

Why did mothers always ask about food? Every time Henry went to his father and stepmother's house for the weekend, the first thing Mom asked when he got home was if he had eaten enough. Like his father didn't have a refrigerator or an oven or a cereal cupboard.

"Henry, are you there?"

"Yes, Mom." He turned to Jake, whose eyes were fixed on the road.

"Take this opportunity, Henry."

What the heck was she talking about?

"Take all these miles between you and the mountain and use them."

Henry still didn't know what she was talking about.

"This South American bird has a distinctive look, with feathers on top of its head that fan into a bold crest when it feels threatened."

"What's a harpy eagle?" said Henry without even thinking.

"What?" said Mom.

"What is an ibis?" said the contestant.

"Wrong," said the game show host. *"The correct answer is 'What is a harpy eagle?'"*

Jake turned to look at Henry. "Nice job," he said.

"Brae misses you already—" Mom's voice cut back in over the game show host.

At the mention of Brae, Henry refocused his attention. "Is he okay?" he said.

"He's fine. Nopie came over after school to play with him."

"Stupid Nopie! Mom don't let—"

"Don't worry about Brae and me," said Mom, interrupting. "We're okay."

Henry put his hand across his knees to quiet them. "I gotta go, Mom," he said. "Bye." And he clicked off the phone before she had a chance to say anything else. He handed it back to Jake.

"You okay?" Jake asked.

"*This means having two toes directed forward and two toes directed backward, as the parrot has.*"

"What is *zygodactyl?*" answered Henry.

"You're real good at those animal questions," said Jake.

Henry felt his face flush. He shrugged. But it was true. He could keep track of animal facts. He liked to do it. He liked animals. They were dependable. They were loyal. When they bit you, it was for a good reason. "You're real good with animals," said Jake. Henry's cheeks flushed again. "You should be the one searching for Tiger." Jake touched the silver baseball. It flickered in the light.

Was the baseball a good-luck charm? Did Jake wish on it?

Henry slouched in his seat and reached his leg toward the rearview mirror. He touched the baseball with his foot. He wished like a parrot with its zygodactyl-like toes, forward and backward. He wished forward that Tiger would find his way home, and that he would find his marble in New Orleans. He wished, backward—with every bone in his body—that he could let Wayne win that last race down the mountain.

Zavion figured out how to get to New Orleans.

The clown brothers had helped him.

"Why'd the bird NOT cross the road?" Skeet said.

"Why?" asked Tavius and Enzo in unison.

"Because it couldn't swim!" Skeet hooted. "Get it? The street had been flooded with water? And it couldn't swim?"

"But it could fly," said Tavius.

"Yeah, birdbrain," said Enzo.

Zavion had been making bread at the time. He was on the thirty-sixth knead when Skeet told his joke, and he had laughed out loud, almost losing count.

"Count me in for a piece of that bread," said Tavius. "Honey oat with a heaping spoonful of guffaw!"

"Food for the heart," said Enzo.

"Food for the soul," echoed Skeet.

As Zavion folded and pushed and turned and folded the

dough, he laughed again, thinking about the bird joke. He liked the clown brothers.

Why'd the bird NOT cross the road?

Ha!

Aha!

Birds! The bird lady. Diana. She went to New Orleans all the time. Maybe he could hitch a ride with her.

The marble on the windowsill *was* a good idea. Zavion had slept a little better. And now he had the first idea for his plan.

Osprey ran into the kitchen, flying a green Converse sneaker on her leash like a kite. The sneaker bounced on its heel on the floor and hit Ms. Cyn's leg. Two mugs slipped from her hands.

The sound of ceramic shattering.

The smell of coffee splattering against the cupboard.

The crash rattled something in the back of Zavion's brain.

All of a sudden, Zavion couldn't breathe.

He was underwater.

He gasped.

"I'm sorry—"

Zavion didn't know if he said those words out loud or not.

* * *

"Lordy, child—" Was Ms. Cyn talking to Zavion or Osprey?

Zavion snapped back. He waited for her to add *You scared the living pee out of me*, but she didn't this time.

"Coffee down," said Enzo.

"That'll keep the snakes away," said Tavius.

"Hush, you," said Ms. Cyn. She wiped coffee off the cupboard.

Zavion picked up pieces of the broken mugs.

"Osprey," said Enzo, "you need to be more careful."

"Watch out, Osprey," said Skeet, "he's going all father-figure on you."

"I *am* her father," said Enzo. He hugged Osprey, who squirmed in his arms.

"Poor kid," said Tavius.

Osprey broke free from Enzo and ran around the kitchen table.

"Poor father," said Zavion.

The clowns laughed.

Zavion had told a joke that made them laugh.

Enzo stood up. "Let me help, Ms. Cyn," he said. Osprey ran a lap around him.

"You've got your hands full," she said.

Zavion straightened up, his own hands full of shards of ceramic mug. "I can take Osprey for a walk," he said.

He wasn't sure why he offered.

Osprey stopped running. "We can take Green for a walk," she said.

"Green?" asked Tavius.

"My dog," she said, pointing to the sneaker.

"Cute pup," said Skeet.

Enzo blinked his eyes a few times fast. Tavius and Skeet immediately threw their arms around him. Zavion remembered that their real dog, Crow, had died in the hurricane. He felt a wave of sadness for Enzo.

"I used to babysit at home," offered Zavion again.

"Go on," said Ms. Cyn. She rinsed her dish towel in the sink. "Get on out of here so I can clean up."

"You?" said Tavius.

"Clean?" said Skeet.

"The kitchen?" said Enzo, grinning. To Zavion, he said, "Thank you."

Osprey stopped at the corner.

For someone with such short legs, she was fast.

"This way," said Zavion. It had occurred to him as they began their walk that he could investigate the bird lady while they were at it. He was pretty sure he knew the way to her house.

"Nope," said Osprey. She turned in the opposite direction

and began skipping down the block. "Sorry, Zavion," she sang over her shoulder. "Green is dragging me this way."

Zavion jogged down the block after her. "Hey! Hold up—"

But Osprey only sped up. "Green!" she yelled. "You know how dogs are—" Her voice was hard to hear now. She was so far ahead of him.

Zavion caught up to her and grabbed the leash. "Whoa," he said, playing along. "C'mon now, Green. Ease up."

Osprey giggled and stopped running. Then she flopped onto the sidewalk. "Green's tired. He needs to rest."

Zavion was tired too. He sat down next to Osprey.

"What am I going to do with you?" he said.

Osprey scooped Green into her lap and rocked the shoe. Osprey reminded Zavion of Mama all of a sudden. He didn't want to remember Mama right now. Right here. For the second time that day, sadness washed over him like a wave.

The wave must have gotten Osprey wet too because she said, "I love Green, but I loved Crow just a little bit more." She turned to Zavion, her eyes wide. "Is that okay to say?"

"Oh, yes," said Zavion. "That makes sense." He reached out and patted Green. "Green is great, but Crow—I bet he was amazing."

Osprey nodded. "He was. Uncle Skeet gave him to me. When Mama was just getting sick. He was a puppy when I got him, but a big puppy! And he would sit on my lap! Uncle Skeet hauled him off me the first time he plopped down, but I kind of liked it. I kind of liked it a lot."

"You did?"

"Uh-huh."

"He didn't knock the breath out of you?"

Osprey giggled again. "A little. But I liked it. I told Uncle Skeet I liked it. He told me Crow must have thought his job was to make sure I didn't float away."

"I bet you didn't, under all that dog," he said.

"Nope." Osprey leaned in toward Zavion. "But you want to know a secret?"

Zavion nodded.

"Dogs are a magic. Sometimes Crow would sit next to me, and only his tail was on my lap. And I *still* didn't float away." Osprey's face looked so serious. "Uncle Skeet told me that anyone whose Mama floated up into heaven needed a dog to keep her from floating up too." Osprey hugged Green to her chest. "But Uncle Skeet and me—we forgot that Crow needed a cat—"

Zavion was puzzled. "A cat?"

Osprey nodded. "To keep him from floating away."

Another wave, and another and another. Zavion stood up so he wouldn't get so wet and took Osprey's hand and pulled her up too. As they walked down the block, Zavion thought about how he wanted a dog now. He wanted Mama to have a dog. He wanted every single person in New Orleans to have a dog, and their dog a cat, and the cat a rat, so that they all could stop floating away—

Zavion wondered if a mountain could keep a person from floating away too.

He believed it could.

A van was parked in the driveway of a blue house in the middle of the street. Birdcages were littered all around it. They were all empty. He walked down the driveway.

"This must be it. 'Diana's Parrot Rescue,'" he read off the side of the van. He stood still for a moment, not sure what he should do.

"Look at what I taught Green!" Osprey sang out.

"Shhhhhhhhh," said Zavion, rushing back to her.

"Watch!" She ran down the driveway, dropped her leash, and then ran back to Zavion. She pulled a peanut out of her pocket and threw it at the sneaker. "Fetch, Green!" The peanut landed next to Green, on the driveway. "He's still learning," she said.

Zavion walked tentatively toward Osprey and then continued inside the garage. "Wow—it's like a bird arcade in here." More cages were stacked inside, all of them filled with birds.

Parrots, macaws, cockatoos, cockatiels, parakeets—there must have been fifty birds altogether. Zavion knelt in front of a cage and put out his finger. A green bird snapped at it. "Okay, boy. Easy does it. I won't bother you, okay?"

Zavion walked out of the garage and straight up to an open window around the side of the house. He cupped his hands around his eyes and peered in. "Wow," he whispered. "There are birds everywhere."

Besides the birds, a person was sleeping on a couch. Two other people were awake. A woman was sitting in a chair, and a man was on a sleeping bag on the floor.

"When are we going back in?" said the man. He rubbed his eyes with his fingers.

"Two hours," said the woman.

A parrot squawked from inside the garage. The sound was low and gravelly, like it was clearing something from his throat.

And there was another sound.

Also gravelly. Truly gravelly. Like something was actually being dragged across a gravel driveway. Like a green sneaker. He had forgotten for a moment that Osprey was with him. He ran to join her.

"You know what we should do, Osprey?" He put his hand on her shoulder to guide her down the driveway. He didn't want her stopping to throw a peanut.

"What?"

"We should get Green a sock so that he has something to keep him from floating away."

Osprey started running down the street. "Floating like this?" she called over her shoulder.

"That's more like running," Zavion said to himself before taking off after her. He hadn't done it in a long time but his leg muscles remembered how. "Yes, like that," he yelled.

And then he followed Osprey and her running, floating dog.

When they got back to the house, Ms. Cyn was sitting in the living room knitting her endless scarf.

"Zavion, honey," she said. She pulled a five-dollar bill out of her pocket. "Here." Zavion said no, but Ms. Cyn insisted. "You did Enzo a big favor," she said. "And I can tell Osprey had a good time. Good times are worth a lot these days. More than this. But it's what I've got and I want you to have it." She pressed the crisp bill into Zavion's hand.

And like that, Zavion had not only figured out how he was going to get to New Orleans, but how he was going to pay back Luna Market for the chocolate bars too.

He had a plan.

He had money.

He had two hours.

*   *   *

Zavion walked to the end of the block and turned the corner. He hitched Tavius's backpack higher on his shoulder. Tavius had been nice to let Zavion borrow it.

For a long walk, Zavion had said. Papa had been busy painting his slate roof shingles and barely looked up when Zavion told him he was going out.

Zavion had paused for a moment, his backpack slung over his shoulder. He had stared at Papa, his fingers gripping the small paintbrush, so intent on making such small lines. Papa's hand shook as he painted a green vertical stripe, maybe a stalk of grass, maybe a stem of a flower. He put the paintbrush down, massaged his hand, and picked it right up again.

Papa was determined.

Zavion was determined too.

Clouds hung in the sky, but just lazy and lounging, no threat of rain. The bread he had packed for his snack jostled inside and clunked him on his back. He put his hand in his pocket and felt the marble. He put his other hand in his other pocket and felt the five-dollar bill. He had left a note for Papa, he had food, he had money, he had a magic marble.

He was ready.

The van was still parked in the driveway. Good. That was

good. He could hear the chatter of the birds in the garage all the way from the street. Zavion strained his ears to hear.

Go, go, go, go.

Did Zavion really want to go through with this? He could turn around. He could walk back to Skeet's house. He could try to forget about the chocolate bars.

But he knew he couldn't forget.

The rows of rooftops sticking out of the water like alligator heads. People stuck, stranded on those monstrous heads. Screaming for help.

Zavion couldn't forget any of it.

A breeze blew in and Zavion glanced at the sky. *Please no wind, please no rain.* He wasn't sure, but he didn't think he had much time to spare. Diana would come outside soon. He had to walk down the driveway now or never. The breeze got bored and left just as quickly as it came.

A bird squawked louder than the others, from somewhere in the garage.

Go!

"Okay, then," Zavion said to the birds.

He snuck a look back up at the sky. Did it look a darker shade of blue? A gray shade of blue? *If I get to New Orleans,* he thought, the words ricocheting against the inside of his skull *then the sky will brighten up, it will turn back to blue—*

A door slammed.

"No! No no no no no—" Zavion spit the pinball words out loud.

He could not get caught.

He could not go back.

Zavion switched gears. He stopped thinking and began to move. Someone had put two birdcages just outside the door to the house and gone back inside.

Zavion ran to the van. He tried the handle. The door slid open. Piles of blankets were on the floor. A cardboard box filled with flashlights sat in one corner. There were feathers everywhere. Zavion buried himself under a green blanket, and slid the door shut.

He poked his head back out. He could feel the static electricity in his hair.

"Not bad. I could pass for junk," he said to himself. The same bird from the garage squawked and set off a chorus of beaked chatter. "The birds agree."

The door to the house slammed again.

A woman was walking toward his side of the van. Zavion wedged himself between a cage and the sidewall. He breathed in. The banket smelled like a wet dog.

The driver's side door opened, and he heard someone put something on the passenger seat. Then the door closed again.

Zavion flattened his body against the floor. Something metal was digging into his rib. He reached his hand under the blanket and pulled out an ax. Oh, what was he doing? He took a deep breath and tried to settle himself more comfortably on his side. His nose caught a whiff of something different than the wet dog smell. Chocolate? Caramel? He hoped his stomach wouldn't rumble and give him away. He sneezed.

Oh boy oh boy oh boy—

Voices came close and then closer. The back door to the van opened.

Oh boy oh boy oh boy oh boy—

"Do we have enough cages?"

"It's all we can fit."

The pinging sound of metal hitting metal rang in Zavion's ears. He felt a cage hit the bottom of his sneaker.

"Do you think the guards will let us through the checkpoint this time?"

Oh boy.

They were going to New Orleans. Zavion was going to New Orleans.

Now.

"Probably. And if they don't, I already put the rest of the brownies in the front seat."

"Good thinking."

"None of them are getting any home cooking right about now. Come to think of it, I should have made a whole meal."

"Uh, Ma—your cooking isn't all that good—"

"Oh hush." And then the door slammed.

Zavion's plan was unfolding. The opposite of kneading bread, it was unfolding, turning and unfolding some more. He fought an urge to yank the blanket off his body. He wanted to stack the cages, throw the blanket over them, and sit on the very top. He thought he would be braver about going back to New Orleans if he could travel by mountain, not by van.

The two front doors opened, and the woman and her son got inside.

"We shouldn't wake Dr. Burke?" the son asked.

"No, let her sleep. She was up all night tending to the birds. And she'll have more to take care of when we come home." The woman started the van. "Are you ready?" she said to her son. The tires crunched down the driveway.

I'm ready, thought Zavion.

chapter 28

HENRY

"**Are you ready?**" said Jake.

"I'm ready," Henry said.

But he wasn't so sure.

Guards let them cross the Crescent City Connection Bridge into New Orleans. It was unlike anything Henry had ever seen. The sun was blazing down, but everything was gray. The street was gray. The houses on the street were gray. Their windows and doors were gray. The cars on the street pointed in all different directions. They were gray too.

HELP ME was painted on the side of one of the houses. An enormous tree branch was partway through the front window of the house next door. At the house across the street, a hole had been ripped out of the roof.

And rows of refrigerators were duct-taped and lined up on the sidewalk. Refrigerators! Henry realized that the sun was so bright because there were barely any trees on the street. There were more refrigerators than trees! He imagined the woods behind his house, imagined them filled with appliances. A stand of washing machines, a path through some dishwashers, a field of microwaves and toasters.

It was unlike anything he had ever smelled either. *Jeezum Crow!* Nopie had pushed him into the dumpster behind the school once. Not on purpose—Nopie wouldn't have dared do that, but Henry had been balancing on its rim and Nopie ran into it with his bike and knocked him in. New Orleans smelled worse than that. Like rotting vegetables and sweat and sour milk. Like the entire city was a giant dumpster.

Henry breathed in deeply. The thick air coated his lungs, his head, and his thoughts like glue.

He remembered Wayne's funeral. The way his body had come unglued. The way it had exploded into little bits all over the church.

They drove for a few blocks in silence. The only other vehicles on the streets—besides the pickup sticks array of cars facing every which way—were a Humvee, two construction vehicles, another eighteen-wheeler, and a truck pulling a boat.

"You okay?" said Jake.

Henry nodded. He couldn't speak.

"Keep your eye out for a sign. We need to find Camp Street. This might even be it."

Henry nodded again.

They crossed an intersection.

A Chevy Blazer sat parked in front of a house. Or what was left of the house. Magnets covered the car, from the hood to the back bumper, from the wheels to the roof.

"Can you stop?" Henry managed to say.

Jake stopped the truck and Henry got out. He walked over to the Chevy.

There were hundreds of magnets covering it.

I ♥ NEW ORLEANS.

An American flag.

A yellow smiley face.

Mickey Mouse.

Advertisements for doctor's offices, law firms, electricians, and towing companies.

And photos.

So many photos. School pictures, pictures of grandparents and grandkids, and animals.

Dogs and cats and birds.

Henry touched a picture of a small girl with pigtails sitting next to a huge dog. The dog was practically sitting on her. He traced the outline of the dog's body.

A tall man with a beard walked over to join Henry.

"What am I doing, right?" the man laughed. "I know. I'm asking myself the same question."

Jake joined Henry and the man.

"I'm an artist. And I haven't been able to paint," he said. "I couldn't just leave them on these refrigerators out here— It seemed like a crime to abandon them—" He opened up his hand. A magnet of Frosty the Snowman sat in his palm. "Maybe I'm just crazy—" he laughed. "You want to put this one on the car?"

Henry took the Frosty magnet. He studied the mosaic of tiny bits of people's lives. Finally he placed the magnet on the front passenger door. Next to a magnet of a quote on one side—JUST WHEN THE CATERPILLAR THOUGHT THE WORLD WAS OVER, IT BECAME A BUTTERFLY—and a cartoon of a dog peeing on a man dressed in red pants on the other.

Sixteen hundred miles from home. Smack in the middle of a street filled with garbage, in front of houses chopped open and smeared with paint, in a place where everything was backward, where the inside, like those refrigerators, was outside and where the outside, like that tree through the front window, was inside. In the middle of the worst kind of destruction Henry had ever seen and ever smelled, he felt the strangest sense of comfort. Because for the first time since he had been on the mountain with Wayne, what was outside Henry matched what was inside.

chapter 29

ZAVION

The van pulled up to the checkpoint around lunchtime. The brownies were a big hit with the guards.

"Best thing I've tasted all day," said the first one.

"Yeah," said the second. "Yesterday was a good day too, someone brought a whole roasted chicken."

"Greens and sweet potato too," said the first.

"Good thing you didn't come yesterday, Ma, or you would've been sent home," said Diana's son.

The guards waved them through. Diana started the van back up and drove into the broken heart of New Orleans. The streets were quiet. That was the first thing Zavion noticed. From his hiding place, he couldn't believe how quiet they were. This wasn't the way home sounded. Where were the car radios and church choirs? Where were the marching bands and boom boxes? This was the moon. Even stuck under the blanket, Zavion felt like he was hurtling through space. Endless silent space.

"Stop here," said Diana's son. Zavion heard a rustling of papers. "This is the first house."

Diana stopped the van, and she and her son got out and went around to open the back door. They took the first two cages and slammed the door shut again.

Zavion sat up slowly. He was afraid to look out the window, so he stared at the blanket that had covered him. He brought it up to his nose. The wet dog smell was strong. Zavion wondered if Diana and her son had any dogs. There was a blue feather tucked in a fold in the blanket. What kind of bird did it come from? A parrot?

Zavion dropped the blanket from his face and took a deep breath.

He coughed.

The smell was thick and sharp.

Not wet dog. More like wet hog. Wet, dead hog. Wild and rotting. He shoved the blanket back up to his nose.

He finally turned his head.

He felt a jolt in his chest, like his heart had popped like popcorn. Turned inside out.

A purple car was parked across the street from the van. Parked upside down. Like a Mardi Gras turtle on its back.

Zavion shuddered.

What had he come back to?

He bit down hard on his top and bottom back teeth. Clenched his jaw.

He had a job to do.

He let go of the blanket and climbed into the front seat. He opened the door and got out of the van.

He put his face down low and raised his shoulder so that his nose was just tucked under his t-shirt.

At least the sun was out. Zavion gazed around him. Gray as far as his eyes could see. The world was gray. A strange combination, a dismal gray under the bright yellow sun.

Could he really do this? Now that he was here, he wasn't so sure. He looked down the block. HELP ME was painted on the side of one of the houses. Zavion remembered the man and woman on the roof of the house on his block. With the sign. HELP US.

HELP US.

HELP ME.

What had he been thinking coming back here? Could he really do this? Find the store and pay it back?

He took a deep breath, hitched his backpack up on his shoulder, and squeezed the marble in his pocket. He tried not to choke as the thick air went down his throat.

chapter 30

HENRY

"Hello?" called Jake.

"Coming!" yelled someone from the back room at the Salvation Army.

Henry inhaled the cold air. It was different from the air outside, easier to take into his lungs.

A woman appeared, carrying a cake. "Hello," she said. "Sorry. I was in the kitchen, just finishing up this new idea I had. This." She held up the cake. "It might taste awful. It might taste just horrible. But I need someone to try it. Want to try it?"

"You make it sound so appealing how can we resist?" said Jake.

The woman closed her eyes and put her hand on her forehead. "I did it again," she said.

"Did what?" asked Henry.

"Dragged out the toilet paper—"

"Huh?" The woman was funny. Henry liked her. He liked

the magnet man he had met too. He inhaled again and got a whiff of—cinnamon?

"Stuck my foot in it," she said. "Or shoved my foot in my mouth. Either way. A foot issue. The usual." She grinned. "I'm Cora. How can I help you?"

"I'm Jake, and this is my friend, Henry. Is this five sixty-four Camp Street?"

"Indeed it is," said Cora.

"Then we have a delivery from Vermont."

"Vermont! You all are wonderful. This is the second delivery we've had from your lovely state this week."

Henry's ears perked up. Maybe the marble was here. Wouldn't that be lucky? Wouldn't that make him believe in its luck again? Maybe?

"Should I start bringing in the bags?" said Jake.

"Oh, yes," said Cora. "Thank you. I can help—"

Henry wanted to know where the bags were from the first delivery. "Do you need help unpacking the new stuff in here?" he asked, trying to sound like he didn't care.

"I could use your help outside," said Jake.

"The smell—" said Henry quickly.

"It's overwhelming," agreed Cora. "The whole city stuck its foot in it, didn't it?"

Jeezum Crow! This woman was so cool!

"It smells like cinnamon in here," he said.

Cora beamed. "You can tell? It's in the cake! Oh, I'm so glad you can tell! That's a good sign, right? Maybe the cake tastes good? I know! How about we try a little of it after we work?"

Henry nodded.

"I have a job for you right in here," she said. "I won't ever turn down help. That would be foolish, wouldn't it? I try not to do foolish things if I can help it. Except for the toilet paper thing." She laughed as she walked toward the door. "Some of the bags are there, behind the counter," said Cora pointing. "And some are on the floor in front of those shelves. Can you take out the clothes and organize them by size?"

As soon as Cora and Jake were outside, Henry ran behind the counter. Three garbage bags were pushed under it, just beneath the cash register. He untied one and pulled out a pair of shorts. Pink. Flowered. Sparkles. *Shoot.* Definitely not from his house.

Now that he was out of Vermont, where life as he knew it had come crashing to an end, now that he was in New Orleans, where he had never been before but where he couldn't totally explain why but he felt like he fit, now that up was down and left was right, he could imagine that anything was possible.

Henry tore open the second bag. T-shirts. He pulled one

out. THE RICHMOND MOUNTAINEERS. Richmond was two towns over. His team played them in football. Got beaten by them most of the time. This bag was not from his house either.

He wasn't sure what he'd do if he found the marble. There was no one to trade it with. Could he wish on it? Wish that Wayne would appear next to him? That time would wind back up like a pitcher getting ready to throw a curveball? That the hole in his skin, the crack in his bone, the tear in his heart, that all his pain would get taped and wrapped and sewn so that it would heal and go away?

He dumped the third bag onto the floor.

Baby clothes!

He kicked into the center of the pile and a pair of tiny overalls flew through the air and landed on the cash register.

Shoot, shoot, shoot!

Henry ran out from behind the counter and over to the shelves Cora had pointed out. Hope filled his fingertips as he pulled a pair of blue jeans out of a bag from between two pairs of corduroys. They were small, but still, he hoped. He reached into the front pocket, wishing, wishing wishing—

There was something there!

He pulled it out with his hand—

Wishing, wishing, wishing—

A car.

A tiny wooden car.

"Finding places to put the clothes?" Cora's voice was muffled behind two huge bags balanced in her arms.

"Huh—?" said Henry. "Uh—oh ... well ... no—" He pushed the car into his pocket.

Cora dropped her bags behind the counter. She surveyed the strewn clothes. "Did you find whatever you were looking for?" She lifted the overalls off the cash register. "Clearly *these* are not your heart's desire—"

"No," said Henry quietly.

Jake came in, arms loaded with boxes.

"A heart's desire is a slippery thing," said Cora. "One minute it's right next door to you, and the next minute it's gone."

"True words," said Jake.

Henry swallowed hard. One minute in your pocket and the next minute on a truck bound south. One minute running down the mountain and the next minute flat on the ground. One minute alive and the next minute dead.

Cora opened the cash register and pulled out a knife.

Jeezum Crow! One minute alive and the next minute dead, all right!

"Would you both be willing to try a piece of my cake?" said Cora. "Please?" She cut into it and that cinnamon smell wafted into Henry's nose. She handed him a slice. "Be honest. I

need it to be perfect. Because"—she leaned in toward Henry—
"here's my secret. This cake is for my heart's desire."

And as Henry took a bite of the cake, which tasted fresh
and delicious and different, and as he spun the tiny wheels on
the small wooden car hidden in his pocket, he wondered if he
would even recognize his own heart's desire if he ran into it on
one of those crazy streets.

chapter 31

ZAVION

Zavion checked the sky. It was a small consolation that there was no rain coming down.

He walked to the corner.

Tulane Avenue and North Broad Street.

He was in Mid-City. Papa had painted a mural at Krescent City Kids day care, which was just around the corner on South Dorgenois Street.

Zavion was hungry. He unzipped his backpack and pulled out his loaf of bread. He ripped off a piece. It tasted like honey.

As he ate, he oriented himself. Gentilly was northeast. Home. Treme was closer. Northeast too. The convention center was southeast. Tulane Avenue would take him close to it.

It was strange. He knew every street and neighborhood like the back of his hand. He knew where he was. But at the same time, everything was different. Upside down. Like that purple car.

Zavion's stomach felt weighed down with the bread he had made. He liked that feeling. Grounded. He needed it because a part of him felt like he was still hurtling through space.

He swallowed his fear with his last bite of bread and took a step into the intersection. He crossed North Broad Street and began to walk down Tulane Avenue. He put his hand in his pocket and closed his fingers around the marble. He imagined its roundness. He suddenly had a thought. The marble had no upside or downside. It was facing the right direction no matter which way it landed. Its feet were on the ground all the time.

Zavion liked this thought. He held on to it and on to the marble as his feet continued down the street.

chapter 32

HENRY

Fueled by peanut-butter-chocolate-cinnamon cake, Henry was now on a full-fledged mission. He was going to find that marble. It wasn't in this Salvation Army, he was sure of it. But there must be more than one Salvation Army in New Orleans.

Jake and Cora were outside getting more boxes. Henry could slip out now. He opened the door and turned to walk down the block.

"And just where do you think you're going?" said Jake. He dropped a stack of boxes on the ground.

"Nowhere." All of a sudden, the center of Henry's stomach, where the cake sat, began to get warm. Like he was baking it all over again.

"Hey, I'm teasing," said Jake.

"Oh, uh—" Henry took a few steps backward.

"We could use your help here." Jake reached out and punched Henry lightly in the arm. "Strong kid like you."

"I don't know...." Henry's belly was getting warmer.

Cora came up from behind Jake. "I promise another treat after you grab a few boxes," she said. "I've got plenty of cake experiments in the kitchen."

"A bunch of garbage bags are sitting right at the edge of the trailer. Go on and get those, Henry," said Jake. "Okay?"

"No." Henry's belly was hot now. *Oh man!* Why wouldn't Jake just let him go?

"No?"

"No!" Like a match striking the side of a box, the *no* ignited him.

"Henry." Jake reached out to touch Henry's arm. "I can't let you wander around without me."

"Let go of me!"

"What's going on?" Jake tightened his grip. His eyes looked into Henry's. They darted back and forth, searching for something.

Henry couldn't look at him. Henry turned from Jake to Cora. Cora's eyes were wide and deep. Henry thought he saw understanding swimming in them, but he couldn't be sure. All he knew was that the fire inside him flickered.

"Henry?" Jake said gently.

Henry wanted to try to explain the fire to Jake. He really wanted to—

"What is it, Henry?" Jake asked.

No! He couldn't tell him. Before he knew it, he'd yanked his arm away from Jake and pushed him, with both hands, in the chest.

The spot in his belly blazed.

"What are you doing, Henry?" said Jake.

"What am I doing?" he yelled.

"Yeah, what was that you just did?"

"What am I doing?" Henry yelled again. "What am I doing here?" He flashed on Mount Mansfield. Its hulking body ripping itself from the earth and somersaulting, upside down, right-side up, chasing him. He shook his head like a dog. He didn't know how he would ever get the mountain to release him. "What am I doing here?" he said again. "I'm ... I'm *not* being there!"

And then he ran, ran as fast as he could, ran to get away from Jake, ran like Jake and Cora were the ones burning him, ran to push the aching feeling from his heart into his legs. But no matter how much he ran, or how much he stayed, he couldn't seem to get rid of it.

chapter 33

ZAVION

Tulane Avenue was empty except for a group of people huddled together on the stoop of one yellow house. Their heads were below a brown waterline that cut across the front of the house, slashing the red front door right in half.

Zavion raised his hand in some sort of greeting. One person waved back. A woman. A baby sat on her lap, so maybe she was a mother. No one else even acknowledged Zavion. It was like they didn't see him.

He crossed South Rampart Street. The Mississippi River was only a few blocks away. The convention center was even closer.

Zavion gripped his backpack tighter.

He bit down on his back teeth so hard a pain shot through his jaw all the way to his ears.

It was awful being back in New Orleans. It made Zavion's pulse beat faster. He could feel it at the side of his head. With each thump an image pumped through his body.

Thump. The cross from St. Mary's Church.

Thump. The seat of a playground swing.

Thump. A lamp. *Thump.* A keyboard. *Thump.* A clear suitcase filled with Matchbox cars.

A parade of objects knocked and darted and careened through him. He hadn't remembered seeing them, but he was sure, now, that he had. They had rushed by as he and Papa had made their way through the flooded streets.

He wondered if Joe the photojournalist had taken pictures of them.

Zavion needed to slow down his pulse. If he could slow down, if he could grab hold of the images flooding his body, if he could line them up like his lunch sandwiches in the refrigerator, neat and organized in a row, he knew he would feel better. He rubbed the side of his head.

Lamp, next to—

Keyboard, next to—

Matchbox suitcase, next to—

Boot.

But it didn't work. How could it? At the intersection, where he had stopped, a group of refrigerators stood together on the corner. With all these broken refrigerators littering the street, there was no hope for keeping sandwiches lined up straight and fresh.

Still, he tried again.

Boot, next to—

Teddy bear, next to—

Soup pot, next to—

Kite—

The memory hit Zavion like a bucketful of marbles.

An orange kite.

A blue sky.

A long white string.

Little hands.

Zavion's hands.

Big hands.

Mama's hands.

A gorgeous fall day, just the right amount of wind, not too hot and not too cold. Zavion and Mama in Pontchartrain Park, flying the brand-new kite he got for his birthday. He begged to fly it alone and immediately snagged it on a branch and ripped it.

"I'm sorry, Mama," he whispered. "I'm sorry, I'm sorry, I'm sorry—" He said it over and over again until Mama's arms had opened wide.

"It was a kite," she said. "And you were you. Now it is a torn kite"—she put her hands on Zavion's cheeks—"and you are still

you." She hugged him so hard they fell over, laughing. They lay on their backs and watched the kite dance against the clouds.

It wasn't the first time she told him about Grandmother Mountain, but it was the time he remembered.

"Grandmother Mountain was only a small pile of rocks and some dirt and a few red spruce trees at first," Mama said, waving her hand slowly from side to side as she guided the kite in the air. "Every time she stopped wandering, she grew. In the valley, she found more dirt. By the river, she found more rocks. By the time she came upon Grandfather Mountain, she was a grand mountain. But she still found something when she put down her roots to be near him." Mama squeezed Zavion's arm with her free hand. "Just like I did with your papa. I wandered into New Orleans, all grown up like a mountain, but I found the one last thing I was missing—someone to be connected to"—she stood up, reaching out her hand to Zavion—"and then I found you—someone to love more than anything in the whole entire world...."

Zavion squeezed the marble for luck, for luck and to quell the fear that was uncurled and loose and roaming through his body.

Zavion had to find Luna Market.

He began to run.

HENRY

Henry ran and ran and ran—

chapter 35
ZAVION

Zavion ran and ran and ran—

HENRY

A boy turned onto the block. Henry caught him out of the corner of his eye. He had long legs, and a backpack bounced against his shoulder. The boy caught up to Henry. They ran side by side for ten strides or so—

Henry was back on the mountain—

Racing Wayne—

The boy sprinted ahead.

The boy tried to jump over a tree that had fallen across the sidewalk.

His jeans got caught on a branch and he pitched forward, falling on his hands.

Henry watched him wrench himself free and keep on running.

He looked like he was running for his life.

chapter 37

ZAVION

Zavion saw the concrete sidewalk.

It looked like the moon close up.

Small craters and drifts of gray-brown mud.

He smelled it too.

He had to. It was half an inch from his nose.

Musty, old water.

He scrambled to his feet and kept running. A stride and a burn in his lungs and thighs that he knew so well.

At the next corner he looked up.

Canal Street and Camp Street.

He was getting close to Luna Market.

As he crossed the intersection, he had the strange feeling he was being followed.

Was it fear, uncurling its long, cold body, following him down the street?

He looked back over his shoulder.

A boy was running behind him.

He looked like he was running for his life.

chapter 38

HENRY

Henry ran until his legs gave out. He didn't know if Jake and Cora were following him, but his calves cramped up and he couldn't run another inch. He leaned over his knees, breathing in gulps like he was drinking water from the river. He walked like that, bent over, down a short walkway to a house and sat, without ever straightening up, on its porch step.

Henry leaned back on his elbows and looked up at the sky. It matched the ground, the houses, the street, the few trees, and, mostly, the garbage.

Gray.

All of it was gray.

And flat.

Henry heard a rumbling sound. He sat up and looked down the street. Three boys were skateboarding. The boy in the front—a short kid wearing a black t-shirt and black jeans— jumped onto the sidewalk and skated toward the fallen tree.

Henry watched him bend his knees, grab the front of his board, and jump the tree. The other two followed him. Then they skated back onto the street, picked up speed, and were gone.

Did they race on their skateboards? Did they have a fourth friend? Where was he?

Henry wondered what their story was.

chapter 39

ZAVION

Help—

A thousand voices calling for help flooded through Zavion.

He couldn't tell if the sounds were coming from inside him or out on the street. He stopped running, stopped walking, and then stood still.

Help—

He looked around but didn't see anyone on the street.

Fear was back. He knew it had been waiting for him, curled up in a tight ball. Zavion couldn't tell if it had been hiding in the rubble of New Orleans, camouflaged in mud and trash, or if it had been lodged in his own body, tucked small and hard at the corner of his lower rib.

But it was back. Long and cold. It stretched from Zavion, to the stop sign on the corner, and wound around back to his body.

Zavion stared at the gray street. At the gray neighborhood.

He listened to the silence, now that his heart had stopped blasting. *Please let there be some sound,* he thought. *Please let there be some movement.* But there was nothing. Only the fierce sun pushing down on a city ripped open, top to bottom, organs and veins and muscles torn away, with its bones exposed to the harsh light.

And what did that make Zavion? A lone cell, flung far, gasping for breath, lost, lost, lost.

Fear was definitely back.

But Zavion had made it to Luna Market.

Its window was taped up with a piece of cardboard and half the space was dark, but the lights were on in the front and Zavion could see a woman carrying a box down an aisle.

Okay, then.

They would walk in together.

He and Fear.

He reached into his pocket and touched his marble.

He would stand here for a few minutes, until he could walk in as a trio.

Zavion, Fear, and a Magic.

chapter 40

HENRY

"Help—"

A muffled voice called from somewhere.

Henry's heart froze, and what was already quiet became silent.

He instinctively reached his hand into his pocket to touch the marble. But of course it wasn't there.

"Help—"

The voice sounded louder.

Henry leaned forward and peered into the street. Had one of the skateboard boys called out?

"Help— Hello—"

The voice was coming from inside the house.

A switch flipped in Henry's heart, and he felt the rush of blood pumping through his body all the way down to his feet, which began to move without Henry even thinking about it. He walked up the porch steps and into the house.

Jeezum Crow!

Water had pushed up through the subfloor in the entryway. And the subfloor had pushed up the tiles above it so they were frozen in wavelike shapes, some up and some down. A long narrow rug that lined the hall just past the entryway was covered with a thick brown sludge.

Henry stumbled over the tiles and sank into the muck on the rug. The living room was just past the hall. Or he thought it was the living room. He couldn't quite tell. A desk and a bookcase and a—was it a washing machine?—had risen up from their spots on the floor and floated across the room. Dropped back down somewhere strange and new. Chairs were on their sides, broken in half. A table was turned upside down and looked like a turtle, its legs stuck helplessly in the air. Henry thought of Nopie on his back, silver boots flailing. The shelves from the bookcase were scattered around the room and the books were almost disintegrated, globs of white mush, like snow.

Henry walked around the rest of the downstairs. There was a coffee table in the kitchen. Another bookcase laid across the bathroom door. A lamp on the stairs, a rug on the couch, a toaster in the hall. A big armchair, a trunk, a piano, fans, French doors. All strewn across the house like a giant hand had scooped them up and tossed them back down without caring where they landed.

A brown watermark ran in a horizontal line around the entire first floor. After he had checked everywhere for the voice, Henry began to climb the stairs. He imagined the water rising. The water climbing the stairs one by one. He followed the watermark.

He slipped. There was so much mud.

In the corners of the stairs, the mud was thick with pieces of rock and grass and garbage. Henry stepped over what he thought might be part of a dead snake. He stood quietly for a moment when he reached the second floor.

"Hello. Hello. Hello. Hello—"

Henry found the room the voice was coming from and opened the door.

He scanned the room. A dresser on its side. A broken window. A closet door off of its hinges. A chair. A bed.

No one.

But clothes were laid out on the bed for work, or school.

Henry got down on his knees and looked under the bed.

No one.

He walked over to the closet and picked up a pile of clothes.

No one.

He scanned the room again. The dresser. The window. The closet door. The chair. The bed—

"Hello—"

—a birdcage.

A birdcage with a cloth thrown over it sat on the floor next to the foot of the bed.

Henry lifted the cloth. Underneath was the most beautiful bird he had ever seen. A parrot. With a brown head the color of the woods behind his house, twelve shades of brown, and a bright yellow band around his neck, a lime-green chest, and stripes along his back. Stripes. A tiger parrot. He had never seen a live one before. It stared right at Henry, its deep brown eyes piercing his.

"Hello," he said again. "Help, would'ja? You wash the dishes and I'll sweep the floor."

Henry hadn't realized he was holding his breath. It tumbled out with laughter. "Okay, okay, I'm here to help you, buddy," he said.

To Henry's left, a blanket lay on the floor. Two glasses and an empty bottle were tipped over on top of it. Two plates sat empty at either end. Henry scanned the rest of the room. Mud, watermarks, furniture in strange places. All things he had already come to expect. But the bed looked weird. He leaned against it. There were pieces of paper taped onto each back bedpost.

"What are those?" asked Henry.

The bird didn't answer.

He untaped them and sat down on the bed to read.

"They look like wishes," said Henry. He talked to the bird. "What your people wanted their family to know. They had some money in the bank. Ooooh, and some under the mattress." He lifted it. "They must have taken their stash." He scanned the papers. "Tiger was supposed to go to their daughter."

"Your name is Tiger, buddy?"

"Tiger's the name, keeping you on task is the game."

Henry stuck his finger in the parrot's cage. In Tiger's cage. Another Tiger. First a cat, and now a bird. "Wow. They didn't think they were going to get out of here alive, did they?"

Henry looked at the blanket and the plates and glasses again. A picnic. It looked like a picnic. Like the one he and Wayne had on the top of Mount Mansfield that night. "Oh man— maybe they thought this was going to be their last meal—"

Wayne's last meal—

Wayne opened his backpack and took out a block of cheese and his sleeping bag. He spread the bag on the ground. Then he lay down on top of it and pushed his pack under his head like a pillow.

"Come here, Brae," he said. Brae lay down along the length of Wayne's body. Wayne tore off two chunks of cheese and fed one to Brae. "You gonna lie down, Henry?"

"I don't think so."

"Brae'll keep you warm. And we can throw your sleeping bag over us too."

"Yeah, right, share my sleeping bag with you—" Henry pushed Wayne with his foot. "Over my dead body."

"I wouldn't want to share your sleeping bag with you and your stinking dead body," said Wayne. He sat up and punched Henry back.

The boys stared straight up into the sky.

"Whoa," Henry said.

"I know," said Wayne. "I take it back. I do feel small up here."

"Help, wouldja?"

Henry pushed his fists into his eyes. Pulsing orange spots. Better than seeing Wayne. He moved his hands from his face. Tiger's head shone in all those shades of brown, his eyes the darkest, like the dirt in the garden after it's been turned. Henry opened Tiger's cage door. He stuck his hand inside. Tiger leaned forward, like he was taking a bow, and touched the tip of his beak to Henry's finger. It was quick and he barely made contact, but Henry felt it. A butterfly landing on his skin and then taking flight.

"C'mon up, Tiger," Henry whispered. He made a soft clicking sound with his tongue. Tiger extended his wings. "C'mon up." He clicked again.

Tiger stepped onto Henry's hand. The bird was amazing. The feathers down his back were striped shiny night-sky black and bright sunshine yellow. Like day and night all at the same time.

Henry scanned the pieces of paper. "Mark McKenzie," he said. "And Maryanne Weidner. They must really miss you."

"Mark and Maryanne. Mark and Maryanne. Can't live with 'em, can't live without 'em," said Tiger. "You sweep the floor, Mark. Ever heard of a broom?"

Henry burst out laughing, and Tiger squawked and flew off his hand. He flapped around the room, a spot of bright light in the gray. He landed on the windowsill.

Henry stood up from the bed. "Come on, boy," he said, stretching out his arm. "Come on back." He pointed to his arm. Tiger cocked his head and then gently landed right where Henry asked him to.

"Let's get out of here," said Henry to Tiger. "Maybe we can find the people who belong to you."

Jake and Cora were walking down the street when Henry came out of the house with Tiger balanced on his arm and the cage in his hand.

"Henry—" Jake's voice was sharp.

"Jake." Henry said his name like a one-word sentence. "I'm—"

But before he could finish his next, slightly longer sentence, Jake pulled him against his chest and hugged him tight.

"—sorry." Henry finished the sentence into Jake's jacket. He really was too.

"I was worried about you, Henry." Jake pulled back and swiped at Henry's hair.

"I was too," said Cora. Her eyes were still wide and deep.

"And who's this?" Jake said, pointing to Henry's arm.

"You won't believe this," began Henry, "but his name is Tiger."

Jake closed his eyes. "One Tiger lost and another one found." He opened his eyes again. "Kind of makes sense, huh?"

Sense? Henry wasn't sure anything made sense anymore.

He swallowed and then coughed. His throat was so dry.

Nothing made sense anymore except that he was thirsty.

"I need a drink," he said.

"You need a drink. Okay. We can take care of that. Maybe." Jake turned to Cora. "Is there a store around here that is actually open?"

Cora nodded. "Luna's back," she said. "She's sort of open. Half the store is, anyway. Tell her I sent you. She'll find you drinks."

"To Luna's, then," said Jake.

Cora pointed. "This is Chartres Street. Keep walking for

another block and a half. Luna Market is just past Bienville Street."

"Thank you," said Jake. Then he stared at Henry for a moment. "I'm glad you're okay," he said. "I can't lose you too."

I can't lose you too.

Henry realized he felt the same way.

chapter 41

ZAVION

Zavion glanced nervously at the sky. It was not a kite-
flying kind of blue or breezy. He looked back down. No use
watching the sky, or even thinking about it. He couldn't stand
out here all day. He had a job to do and he was going to do it.
He squeezed the marble one more time and imagined it was
like a sponge and he was soaking in all its magic.

Zavion walked into Luna Market and went straight to the
checkout counter. A woman with a baby on her hip was buying toothpaste and a toothbrush.

"I used my toothbrush to scrub the grout between my
kitchen tiles," she was saying. "I couldn't take it for another
minute, all that mud left over. The rest of the house is a mess.
Broken windows, ripped-up front porch, shingles gone off the
roof. But my kitchen floor is clean. Spotless. You could eat
off it."

"Good for you," said the cashier. She was an older woman

with long hair pulled back in a scarf and yellow and black bangles up her arm, like tiger stripes.

"But then I needed a new toothbrush," said the woman with the baby.

"You sure did," said the cashier.

Zavion reached into the candy shelf and picked out a handful of chocolate bars. He wasn't going to buy them. Just show them to the cashier so she'd know what he was paying for.

"Maybe I'll scrub the bathroom tonight," said the woman as she walked out. "Maybe I'll be in to buy another toothbrush tomorrow."

"I'll be here," said the cashier.

The woman with the baby held the door open for a boy and a man. A bird sat on the boy's arm. The man walked up to the cashier. The boy and the bird walked down one of the lit aisles.

"You must be Luna," said the man.

"I sure am," said the cashier.

Luna. Luna Market. This was the owner of the market. Zavion could repay the owner.

"It's a pleasure to meet you," said the man. "Cora, over at the Salvation Army, sent us here in search of drinks."

"Bless your soul," said Luna. "And bless Cora's quirky, kind soul too." She laughed a low, rumbly laugh.

Zavion liked the way it sounded, like a cat purring.

Luna turned to Zavion. "You all set, honey?"

Zavion nodded.

He placed the chocolate bars on the counter and then put his hand in his pocket and pulled out everything that was inside. "Here, ma'am." He emptied his hand of the marble and—

—that was all.

Oh boy.

No money.

No!

It must be in his other one. *Yes.* He had put the money in one and the marble in the other. He put the marble back in his pocket and reached his hand into the other one.

No, no, no, no, no—

He had lost the money.

"Do you want these chocolate bars?" asked Luna gently.

"Yes!"

Zavion turned his head. The boy and the bird were behind him. The boy had two sodas in his hand.

"Yes!" the bird squawked again.

"Yes—" Zavion said.

He stared at the cardboard in the window. His mind was just as thick as the board. He couldn't think of what to do.

His heart raced. His palms sweat. He loosened his grip on his backpack and closed his wet fingers around it again. The bread bounced inside.

The bread.

The bread!

"Ma'am?" said Zavion. He took the backpack off his shoulder. He unzipped it. He pulled out the loaf of bread and put it on the counter. He cleared his throat. "Ma'am," he said again, "it's honey oat. Homemade. I made it today."

"It smells delicious," said Luna.

"Can I trade it for the chocolate bars?" said Zavion.

"Oh, honey—"

"Please?" Zavion was desperate. "It's food for the heart and soul."

"Oh, honey," she said again. She looked straight into Zavion's eyes. "Yes. Oh, yes. You can trade it for the chocolate."

Luna took the bread and handed Zavion the chocolate bars.

"No, ma'am," said Zavion. "Those aren't mine." He pushed them over to her.

"But you just bought them," she said.

"No, ma'am, I didn't," Zavion said. He could feel tears welling up in his eyes.

"I don't understand," Luna said. She reached her hands behind her head to tighten her scarf, and her bangles rattled.

The sound rattled something deep in Zavion's brain.

"I owe you this bread," said Zavion, his voice shaking.

"You do?"

"I—during the hurricane—when your store was closed—Papa and I—we—we were hungry—we took—I took—I took—I left an IOU—"

"Can't live with 'em, can't live without 'em," said Tiger, spreading his wings and then closing them again.

"Oh, child," said Luna. Her bangles rattled again. It was a soothing sound, like chimes.

The sound rang a bell in Zavion's brain.

Luna pulled something out from behind the counter. "Are these yours?"

The two roof shingles.

Zavion nodded.

"I understand," said Luna. She took Zavion's hand and pressed the shingles against his palm. Her fingers were soft. "Thank you," she said.

Zavion forced himself to look right into Luna's eyes, like he said he would.

"I'm sorry," he choked out. His jaw came unhinged, and a sob escaped from somewhere deep in his body.

Luna leaned across the counter and put her hand on Zavion's cheek. She held his stare with a soft one of her own.

"It's okay, child. It's okay." She tightened her hand slightly. Her bangles rang right in Zavion's ear.

Mama.

Luna sounded like Mama.

"You're okay," she said. "You're okay."

And in that moment, a window opened inside Zavion's brain. He felt the metal latch turn, felt the rush of air as the crisscross of wood and glass lifted.

chapter 42
HENRY

Henry watched the boy stumble out of the market.

"Beautiful bird," said Luna. Her voice was thick, like she was holding back tears.

"It is, isn't it?" said Jake with the same voice.

Henry knew they were both about to cry because he felt the same way.

"Live and learn, live and learn—" squawked Tiger.

Luna laughed. "But I don't think you're buying this bird now, are you?" she said. "Unless it's new, I don't think I have a bird aisle. But I could, I certainly could. It's a new day, a new world— Why not sell birds—"

Henry laughed too, glad for the distraction.

Jake paid for the sodas.

"Thank you," he said.

"My pleasure," said Luna.

"And good luck."

"Good-bye," said Henry.

"Good-bye, honey," said Luna.

"See ya later, alligator," said Tiger.

"True words," laughed Luna. "As God is my witness, I saw an upside-down alligator by the side of the street on my way to work. It *is* a new world—"

chapter 43

ZAVION

The wind cut through the sky, a sound like scissors through paper.

Zavion glanced up. The dark was getting darker. The wind tore the black away and revealed a blacker black behind it. Rain began to fall. The wind tore into his skin. He felt it rip into his arm and his neck and face, and then felt the sting of the rain. He wasn't sure if his legs would hold him up.

"Hey—"

He heard someone's voice, but he didn't look back.

"Hey—" the voice said. "Are you okay?"

Another rumble. This time it was louder. Zavion's ears began to ring.

"Mama—" he said.

A long, deep cracking sound. Like something being split open. Zavion could barely hear now. There was a flash of lightning. A boy's face—the boy with the bird—shone for a second and Zavion could see his mouth move, but he couldn't hear what he was saying. Zavion felt a hand on his shoulder.

Another cracking sound. Again, something being split open. Was it him? Was he being split open wide? Zavion scrambled up a pile of something by the side of the market. Pieces of a wall. He climbed as high as he could. A musty, windy water smell filled his nose. A levee was crumbling. The wind and the water flooded over him. There was a squealing in his ears. The violin sound. It was back. Mama—

He climbed Grandmother Mountain higher. Zavion put his hands over his ears. He lost his balance. He was falling—

—falling from his attic window, falling onto the door, falling off the door into the rushing, rising water—

"Hey—" A voice cut through the squealing.

Hands grabbed him. Another crack of thunder. In the lightning flash, Zavion saw his own hands gripping the back of someone's shirt. The windy water smell filled Zavion's nose again, and the flooding sensation rose inside his body.

"Hey—" The voice again. "Stay with me here, okay?"

Who was talking to him?

"This isn't a hurricane," the voice said. "You are safe." The person pressed his hand into Zavion's shoulder. "You are safe," he repeated.

"What's happening to him?" Zavion heard another voice ask.

"Hello," said a third voice. "You are safe. You are safe. You are safe." Another crack of thunder. The long, high squeal of the violin. Too close, too close. A bird screeched. And then the levee crumbled to the ground.

"No, I am not! I am not safe!" Zavion tried to stand up, but a hand kept him still.

"You are," the voice said.

"NO! NO ONE IS SAFE! WHERE IS PAPA? WHERE IS MAMA? WHERE IS SHE?"

"Come back here—"

"DON'T YOU SMELL IT?"

"You're okay, son—"

"THE WIND! THE WATER!" He couldn't stop yelling. "WHAT IF I FALL?" Words poured out of him.

"No!" The voice was yelling now too. The person gripped Zavion's arms. "No, you won't fall!" The person turned his head. "Hold on to his other shoulder," he said. The other person knelt down next to Zavion. "Put pressure on him. Let him know you're here."

"WHAT IF I CAN'T BREATHE?"

"You won't stop breathing," said the first voice.

"WHAT IF I DIE?"

"You won't die," said the voice again.

"Jeezum Crow. He's as stiff as a board," came a different, quiet voice next to Zavion.

And like Luna in the market—

—like Mama—

the voice said, "You're okay. You're okay."

chapter 44

HENRY

Stiff as a board.

Just the way Henry had felt that day he biked up and down, up and down, up and down the driveway.

Stiff as a board and frozen.

Frozen with fear.

ZAVION

Another round of thunder and lightning, quieter than before. In the flash of light, Zavion saw tears in the eyes of the person sitting next to him. A man. The man from the market.

"You are safe," he said quietly. He looked Zavion straight in the eyes.

"No, I'm not," Zavion said quietly too. "Not here."

chapter 46

HENRY

The boy's breathing was heavy. He was panting. Like he was Brae. Henry let go of his shoulder and sank back onto the ground.

Not here.

Not here.

Not here.

How many places could be unsafe? For Henry it was the mountain. For this kid it was here. New Orleans. Louisiana.

Henry thought something then.

What if the place came with you?

What if no matter where you went, it followed you?

What if the mountain had followed him?

Or worse, what if it was inside him?

chapter 47

ZAVION

"The storm is over," said the man.

The storm was traveling away from the street—that was true. The violin squeal was slowly fading.

But the memory was getting brighter.

The storm had brought it crashing in.

Luna had opened the window in his brain and the memory had flooded back to him.

He remembered.

Mama's hands on his face.

Mama's voice.

Mama's hug.

A blue ceramic mug.

Mama's mug. Her favorite mug. The one she brought from

North Carolina. It had a tan and brown bird on it, built up with clay, so it stuck out from the rest of the mug. It was positioned at the top, at an angle. Its wings were fully opened.

Zavion remembered tracing the outline of the bird when Mama set it down in the morning to have her cup of coffee. He remembered wondering, each time, if the next time the bird would be gone. If it would ever finally fly away.

Zavion remembered that blue mug, and a sad blue thing crept through the open window in his brain.

It crouched in a corner there.

Then it stretched its body out flat.

Zavion was four.

He had been outside, pulling mint out of the tiny garden Mama kept behind their house. Her family had kept enormous gardens at their house in North Carolina, at the base of Grandmother Mountain, and Mama had carried a garbage bag filled with dirt when she moved. A little bit of North Carolina in New Orleans. Just enough dirt for a tiny garden.

She grew tomatoes, cucumbers, peas, and mint.

Lots of mint.

That morning she had sent Zavion out to pick some for a big pitcher of iced tea she was making.

Mint, ginger, and tea.

Her specialty.

"My special tea," she would say. And then she would laugh.

That low, rumbly laugh like a cat purring.

Zavion picked two big handfuls of mint and was running back into the kitchen. He was so excited he had forgotten to take off his garden boots—tall, yellow rubber boots—just inside the front door, which was a rule of Mama's. She liked a clean floor, liked to walk in the house barefoot, and didn't want to step in dirt or mud or worse.

"New Orleans is dirtier than North Carolina," she always said.

"New Orleans just has more to offer," Papa always said.

"True words," she always said back.

Zavion barreled into the kitchen, his fists full of mint. The mud on the bottom of his boots was slippery. He skidded when he hit the linoleum floor. Hands full, he careened into Mama, who was standing at the kitchen counter, mug in one hand, a piece of ginger in the other.

Zavion banged into Mama with such force that his fists popped open and the mint scattered onto the floor. But that was not the worst part.

Mama's mug, the mug with the bird that was getting ready

to take flight, the one Mama had brought with her from North Carolina, flew into the air—

—like Zavion always thought the bird might—

—and cracked on the muddy linoleum floor.

Shards of blue clay skittered everywhere.

And Zavion felt his own body crack into a million pieces.

He had broken Mama's rule.

He had broken Mama's mug.

He began to cry.

"I'm sorry, I'm sorry, I'm sorry—" he wailed.

Mama knelt down on the floor and took his face in her hands.

"It's okay," she said.

Her bangles sounded like chimes in Zavion's ears.

Then she pulled him into a big, warm hug.

"It's okay," she whispered. "You're okay. You will always be okay."

And then she said what she would say many more times.

"You were you, you are still you, and I love you all the same."

She said it until she died.

And then Zavion never heard it again.

Instead, he shut the window, turned the lock, and vowed never to make a mistake or break a rule again.

*   *   *

Zavion looked at the man whose hand was still on his shoulder. He looked at the boy whose hand was still on his other shoulder. He looked at the bird, who was sitting on the arm of the boy, balanced like he was on a tighrope between them.

He didn't know them.

But, at the same time, he did.

He asked them, "Do you live near a mountain?" A question that he was certain he knew the answer to.

The boy said, "Yes."

And then Zavion said, "I need to go to it."

chapter 48

HENRY

Henry sat back down on the ground.

He wasn't exactly sure what had just happened, but he knew that in the flashes of lightning that illuminated the dark, he had seen pieces of himself.

He also knew that he had helped this boy.

Or maybe, in a way, he had saved him.

Peregrine falcon style.

A bird landed on the sidewalk in front of Henry. A pigeon. It strutted back and forth a few times, pecking at one piece of garbage and then another, until it stopped in front of a soggy, crushed cardboard box. It stuck its head inside and pulled out a piece of something, maybe a cracker or an orange peel.

The boy didn't look so good. His eyes were too wide and his hands were shaking in his lap.

He didn't feel safe. He had said so.

And he wanted to climb Mount Mansfield.

Why?

Henry had been amazed that the boy knew he and Jake lived near a mountain until the boy pointed to his football jersey. MOUNT MANSFIELD JUNIOR FOOTBALL, UNDERHILL, VERMONT was written across his chest. Above a picture of the stupid mountain. How had he not realized that he had carried Mansfield all the way to New Orleans?

Jeezum Crow!

Henry didn't have the heart to tell the boy just how dangerous the mountain was.

Roots sticking up across the trail.

Sharp branches hanging too low.

Rock ledges that dropped onto hard ground.

Henry wasn't ready to go back home.

Tiger hopped off Henry's arm to join the pigeon. He stuck his head in the box and grabbed a banana peel. He pulled tiny strings of pale yellow fruit off the inside of the peel. The pigeon took one from him and ate it.

Henry watched them for a moment, these two birds who had never seen each other before, sharing a strange sort of meal.

*   *   *

Jake, who had been silently holding the boy's shoulder all this time, cleared his throat.

"We should get you home," he said to the boy.

"I need to go to Vermont," said the boy, getting on to his knees. "Please—"

Henry could see that Jake was contemplating the boy's request. Or beg. It was more like a beg.

Jake stood up. He put his hand over his mouth like he was trying to gather his words into his hand.

"First"—he paused—"we have to get you home. Where is home?"

Henry stood up too. He clicked his tongue and Tiger flew to his arm.

This bird was smart.

"Five six one one Arts Street. It's in Gentilly. By Pontchartrain Park." The boy didn't stand up. Instead, he opened his left hand, which had been closed tight around something.

The two roof shingles.

"This is home," he said. "This is all that's left of it."

Henry stared at what was left of Zavion's house and all he saw was Mount Mansfield. The muscles in his legs twitched. His nostrils flared, ready to pull in extra oxygen. He knew that mountain better than anything else in the whole world.

What if he could hold Mount Mansfield in his hand?

Henry instinctively wrapped both arms around himself, which startled Tiger, who flapped his wings fast and flew to the boy. He settled himself on his lap and pecked at a shingle.

"He likes your house," Henry said weakly.

The boy smiled.

And as Henry stood under the slowly brightening New Orleans sky, dragging its foul-smelling air into his lungs, he knew he wanted to take this boy to Mount Mansfield.

Luna came outside the market to bring them a grocery bag filled with coffee, juice and a bottle of wine. She said good-bye to Henry, Jake, and the boy, who had told them his name was Zavion.

"It's Basque," Zavion said. "It means 'bright, new house.'"

Henry had smiled then.

"Mine is German," he said. "It means 'ruler of the house.'"

"Not that he's bossy," Jake said.

They walked back to the Salvation Army, which smelled like burnt toast.

"What happened here?" said Henry.

"I burnt toast," said Cora.

When Jake told her they were taking Zavion back to Baton Rouge, she clapped her hands and told them that her dear friend Pierre ran the Salvation Army there.

"Can you bring a load of clothes to him?" she asked. "It will save him a trip."

"Yes!" Henry said so enthusiastically that Tiger had dropped a feather, madly flapping his wings. Initially, Henry didn't like the idea of taking Zavion to Baton Rouge. He wasn't finished searching New Orleans for his marble. He hadn't even really started. But if deliveries went to Baton Rouge too, he was open to it.

"Your house . . . ," began Cora. She put her hand on Zavion's shoulder. "How bad was the damage? Did you lose a lot of things?" Cora's hand fluttered from Zavion to her mouth. "Oh my goodness, am I asking too many questions? I am, aren't I? I'm sticking my foot in it, aren't I? I'm—"

"It's gone," interrupted Zavion. "My house is gone."

"Oh." Cora breathed in sharply. "I'm so sorry. Just like my neighbor Enzo."

"Enzo?" Henry saw Zavion's face brighten.

"Yes."

"Does he have a daughter named Osprey?"

"Yes!"

"I'm staying with him! And Osprey. And his brothers—"

"The singers!" Cora clapped her hands. "Well, look at that! Just look at what I stuck my foot into this time!" She tapped her toes on the ground and spun in a circle. "I have something else for you to take to Baton Rouge!"

"How did you get to New Orleans?" Henry asked Zavion. They were loading Cora's cake into the truck.

"I stowed away in a bird rescue van," said Zavion.

"So cool," Henry said.

"Wayne would have done that," said Jake.

Henry agreed.

chapter 49

ZAVION

Everyone was there. Papa, Isaac, Enzo, Tavius, Skeet, and Osprey. Ms. Cyn, her knitting needles flying. Papa rushed to grab Zavion as soon as his feet hit the ground. He gave him a tight hug and then a good shake.

"You don't do that. You don't do that to me, do you understand?" he said sharply.

"But—" started Zavion.

"Never. Never again."

"But I wasn't lost—I knew where I was—"

"You knew where you were? What good did that do me?"

"I'm sure you were so worried." Jake had made his way around to the other side of the truck.

Papa turned to Jake and shot him a look that made Zavion wince. "Thank you for bringing Zavion home. But you don't have a clue what I was feeling—"

"Don't have a clue!" said Tiger.

"Shhhhh," said Henry. He stuck the bird's cage behind his legs.

"Don't have a clue, ya bonehead!"

"Tiger," Henry hissed.

Osprey laughed. She squirmed out of Enzo's arms and ran to Henry, dragging Green behind her.

"Nice dog," Henry said. "Looks like he runs fast."

"Thank you," she said, grinning. "His name is Green." She pointed behind Henry. "Nice bird."

"Thanks," said Henry. "His name is Tiger. And I'm Henry."

"I'm Osprey."

"Falcon?"

"No, Osprey."

"Eagle?"

"No, Osprey!"

"Owl?" Henry was laughing now.

"No! No!" Osprey poked Henry in the knee and giggled.

Zavion was amazed. In a matter of seconds, Henry and Osprey had become fast friends.

"If you think you're going on any other damn adventure, Zavion, dump that idea out of your head right now," said Papa. "You're coming with me to Gabe's and I'm attaching you to my wrist with Osprey's leash all the way there. Do you understand me?"

"Papa—" Zavion forced himself to look into his eyes. "Papa—" His voice came out a whisper. He opened his palms. The two roof shingles, chipped and gray, sat in his hands. "This is what's left of our house," he managed to say.

"Sweet Jesus—" Papa's eyes filled with tears.

"Two more canvases for you to paint," said Zavion.

Papa pulled him close one more time.

chapter 50

HENRY

"Let's go inside," said Ms. Cyn. She circled her arms around Tavius and Skeet like she was herding sheep. "Time to eat, don't you think?"

"For someone who hates the kitchen, you sure do like what's inside it," said Tavius.

"Hush," said Ms. Cyn. "Get on in—" She ushered them through the door.

Henry hung back and watched Zavion's father hug him hard. He couldn't hear what he said, but he saw him whisper something into Zavion's ear.

I can't lose you. That was what Henry imagined he was saying. *I can't lose you.*

Henry remembered Jake saying that to him only a few short hours before.

chapter 51

ZAVION

"If there's cake, there's a party!" said Enzo.

"Thank you, Cora!" said Tavius.

"Yes, thank you kindly!" said Skeet.

"And coffee and wine!" said Enzo.

"And juice!" piped in Osprey.

"Thank you, Luna!" said Tavius.

"Yes, thank you kindly!" said Skeet.

"Mind your manners!" squawked Tiger.

Ms. Cyn poked her head into the kitchen. She made the party complete. Everyone from the Baton Rouge house was here and accounted for. Even Pierre had come to join them, plus Henry and Jake from Vermont. Vermont! Here! Zavion couldn't quite believe his luck.

Or maybe it wasn't luck. Zavion was too tired to think. He was just relieved and amazed and overwhelmed by the fact that they were here.

"Hope we aren't keeping you awake," said Jake to Ms. Cyn. "I know it's late."

"It was this bird," said Ms. Cyn. "When he was screaming out that grocery list: milk, cheese, butter, juice, sausage, eggs—"

"Sorry," said Henry.

"Ms. Cyn thought she was having a bad broccoli dream," said Enzo.

"A noodle night terror," said Tavius.

"A nut butter nightmare," said Skeet.

"Very funny, you clowns," said Ms. Cyn as she plunked herself down on a chair. "I wasn't asleep. Do you think I would miss a party? Even one in the kitchen? I was just busy." That was true, her scarf looked like it was a mile long. "I wouldn't miss this"— she gestured with her hand around the room—"for anything."

"Tiger is funny," said Osprey.

"But Ms. Cyn is funnier," said Skeet.

"Hey, y'all," said Ms. Cyn. "Ribbing doesn't officially begin until the sun rises, okay?"

"Okay," said Enzo.

"Maybe," said Tavius.

Skeet paused. "Nah," he said.

Zavion took a bite of Cora's cake. It was the best thing he had ever tasted. Better than the sandwiches he made and lined up in the refrigerator, better than the bread he had just learned to knead and bake, and maybe just as good as Mama's ginger mint iced tea.

Across the kitchen table, Osprey scooped some cake into her hand and held it out for Tiger, who reached his beak down to snatch it up. "Crow's dead," said Osprey, "but you're not dead, Tiger. I like you."

"He likes you too, Osprey," said Henry. "You wanna hold him?" Osprey nodded. "Do you think Green will mind?"

Osprey laughed. She pulled her leash onto the table, and attached to its clip was a small spoon. "This is Silver, not Green." She leaned in toward Henry. "And don't you know, Henry? Silver is only pretend."

Henry clicked softly and pointed to the table. Tiger hopped off his shoulder and landed next to Silver. Osprey imitated Henry's clicking sound.

"That's right," Henry said. "Now hold out your arm." Tiger hopped onto Osprey's wrist.

"Hi, Tiger," she said.

"Hello," he said. Then he leaned over and looked at himself in the silver spoon. "What a beaut!" he said. "What a beaut! Shiny!"

All of a sudden, Enzo hopped up. "Shiny! That reminds me of the woman at the convention center."

"The singing woman?" said Tavius.

"Yeah, remember her? Right before we left?" said Enzo. "Remember what she sang?"

" 'This Little Light of Mine,' " said Tavius. "She was incredible—"

"She walked around the center belting that song at the top of her lungs, and people began to follow her, singing along," said Enzo. "By the time we joined in, we couldn't even see the woman—"

"There was such a long line," said Tavius.

"This little light of mine," sang Enzo, *"I'm gonna let it shine—"*

Tavius joined in.

"This little light of mine, I'm gonna let it shine—"

Skeet began to sing too.

"This little light of mine, I'm gonna let it shine."

Osprey got up too, and marched around the room.

"Let it shine, let it shine, let it shine."

Tavius reached his hand out to Pierre, who took it and began to sing too. Ms. Cyn, Papa, and Jake joined in. Even Tiger flew around the room, singing "shine" in all the right places.

As the song filled the kitchen, Zavion had a thought.

He had made it through a thunderstorm. It hadn't been pretty. But he had made it through to the other side.

That was something.

chapter 52

HENRY

"This little light of mine,

I'm gonna let it shine.

This little light of mine,

I'm gonna let it shine.

Let it shine,

Let it shine,

Let it shine."

The singing was the most beautiful thing Henry had ever heard. Layers of voices, perfectly stacked, but all of them different. Like the wind, the sparrows, and the waterfall on the mountain making music at the same time.

He felt something inside, something different from the hot, fiery feeling he usually had. A tugging feeling. A pulling-toward feeling.

Henry needed to do something. Not fight. Not run. Not

sing. Nobody wanted to hear him sing. But he wanted to be a part of it. He scooped Osprey up onto his shoulders and marched with her.

Enzo picked up something white from the laundry basket on the floor next to the back door. He unfolded a pair of underwear.

"This tighty-whitey of mine, I'm gonna let it shine—" He grabbed another pair and tossed it to Skeet, who picked up the underwear and the new song.

"This tighty-whitey of mine-y," he sang, *"I'm gonna put it on my hiney—"* Enzo tossed four more pairs to Tavius, Pierre, Ben, and Jake.

"This tighty-whitey of mine-y,
  I'm gonna put it on my hiney,
  It looks so fine-y
  Me-oh-mine-y
  My butt's so tiny."

Henry laughed so hard he almost dropped Osprey.

"Put me down!" she was laughing too. Henry lifted her off his shoulders, and she marched over to Zavion and wiggled her way into his lap. He wrapped his arms around her. Henry felt that tugging feeling again. He wanted to do something for Zavion.

He saw Mount Mansfield from Zavion's eyes. From someone who had never seen it before. The way the trees changed from birch to fir to tundra. The view of the valley from the very top. Henry wanted to take him there. He pulled Jake aside.

"I want to take Zavion up Mansfield."

Jake played monkey in the middle with a pair of underwear. Jake caught them and threw them to Tavius. "You do?" he said.

Henry did. He needed to find his marble first. But yes, he wanted to take Zavion up Mount Mansfield just a little bit more than he was afraid to be back there.

chapter 53

ZAVION

The party moved into the living room. Zavion could hear them playing a trivia game.

"What colors can butterflies see that humans cannot see?" Zavion heard Enzo ask.

"Colors on the ultraviolet spectrum," said Henry.

"In what key do flies hum?"

"F."

"Which insect can indicate the temperature?"

"Crickets. They have different chirps for warm and cold." Henry was on a roll.

It sounded like they were having fun, but Zavion stayed in the kitchen to clean up. He dried the inside of a ceramic mug with a dish towel. He stood in the middle of the room, took a deep breath, and then, very quietly, began to sing.

"*This little light of mine—*" His voice cracked. He wasn't a very good singer.

"*—I'm gonna let it shine,*
   Let it shine,
   Let it shine,
   Let it shine—"

chapter 54

HENRY

After the trivia game, which Henry won hands down, everyone drifted off to sleep. But Henry couldn't. He wasn't sure why. It wasn't because he was in a new house. It wasn't because he was without Brae, although he missed him something fierce. And it wasn't because of the new breathing all around him, a chorus of inhale and exhale, inhale and exhale. That was music to his ears.

So was the lone voice he had heard earlier, coming from the kitchen.

Henry hummed the song now. If Zavion could be brave and sing, maybe he could too. He opened his mouth. Took a deep breath. As he held it, he listened again to the in and out, up and down, steady and powerful life all around him. He closed his mouth again. He didn't want to ruin all that beautiful music.

* * *

He climbed up the ladder leaning against the house and pulled himself onto the low roof. The sky was clear and the moon was bright. He could see the whole block from where he sat, identical ranch houses with fenced-in backyards.

"What are you doing up there?"

Henry looked down to see Osprey staring at him, her eyes shining in the dark night.

"Just wanted to climb, I guess."

"Can I climb too?" Osprey put her bare foot on the bottom rung of the ladder.

"Shoot. Hold on." Henry inched his way to the edge of the roof and jumped down. "Okay, you go first and I'll follow you." Osprey's legs moved slowly up the ladder. When she got to the top rung, Henry squeezed around her onto the roof and then grabbed her hands and guided her up. She had the leash wrapped around her wrist.

"You're making me nervous," said Henry. "Sit down, okay?"

"Why'd you come up here?" said Osprey. She squatted next to Henry.

"I dunno. I couldn't go to sleep."

"Me too."

Henry lay back so his head was resting on the roof. Osprey lay down too. A cloud passed in front of the moon, darkening the sky for an instant, like a big eye blinking shut, and Osprey almost disappeared. Then the eye opened again and Osprey came back into view.

"I feel big up here," said Osprey. She wiggled her head up onto Henry's chest, right under his chin. Her hair was spongy and soft. "This is so much better than being inside. Don't you think so, Henry?"

"Yup."

Osprey pointed her finger into the sky and then jammed it into Henry's rib. "Are you going home soon?"

"Owww—yeah, I guess." Henry rubbed his side and Osprey grabbed his hand. He couldn't believe it, but he was going to miss this kid. "I'll send you a picture of Brae," he said.

"Who's Brae? An animal?"

"Yup."

"A pig?"

"Nope."

"A sheep?"

"Nope."

"A cow?"

"Yup."

"A cow?!"

"Yup. Part cow."

"Part cow?!"

"Yup. And part dog."

"A cow-dog?" said Osprey, her eyes getting wide.

"Yup."

"I never heard of a cow-dog."

"Oh, they're very rare. You only find them in Vermont."

Osprey clapped her hands. She unwrapped the leash from around her wrist. "You can put this on Brae, okay? It should go on a real dog. A real cow-dog."

Henry took the leash. It was warm from being in Osprey's hand. "Thank you, Falcon," he said.

Falcon.

The PBS special!

Peregrine falcon!

And the red-breasted goose!

"You want to hear something?" said Henry.

"Yes," said Osprey.

"In the Siberian tundra, the arctic fox is always hungry. They want to eat the red-breasted geese that live there."

"Poor geese," said Osprey.

"Yup. But the peregrine falcons take care of the geese. The falcons know how to fight the fox."

"I like the falcons!"

"Me too. You want to hear something else?"

"Yes."

"The geese take care of the falcons too. I just remembered

that. The geese make a great loud alarm call that warns the falcons when the fox is approaching."

"Oh! I like the geese!"

"Me too," said Henry. "I like the way they work together. It's kind of like ... magic."

"Like a magic!" said Osprey.

A magic.

Henry liked that.

"Zavion has a magic," said Osprey.

"He does? What is it?"

"It's a secret."

A secret.

Henry knew about secrets.

But a secret that was a magic?

"Maybe my leash is a magic, Henry," said Osprey.

"I bet it is," said Henry. He gripped the leash. "I'll take a picture of Brae wearing this and send it to you."

And then he had a flash of an idea. He reached into his pocket and pulled out the tiny wooden car from the Salvation Army. He had almost forgotten he had it. "This is from Vermont," he said. "It's for you."

And he knew, with certainty, that it was.

"And maybe this is a magic too!" squealed Osprey.

She took the little car and then leaned back again on

Henry's chest. She ran the car up and down his arm. "This is where you live," she said, placing the car on Henry's wrist. "And this is where I live," she said, driving it along his arm to his shoulder.

"Not too far," he said.

"Nope."

Henry stared into the sky and the moon stared back at him, watched him as he looked down at Osprey, who closed her eyes and wrapped her arms around him. As he rested his chin on Osprey's head, he felt that tugging feeling again. He imagined that the peregrine falcon and the red-breasted goose felt it tug between them too. It was a funny feeling. Funny, but good. A rooted kind of feeling, pulling him to the ground, even though he was up in the sky.

chapter 55

ZAVION

Up on a ladder, Papa was painting one of the living room walls. Zavion needed to tell Papa that they should go to Vermont with Henry and Jake. He ran his hand down Tiger's wing feathers, felt the muscles under them, felt how strong his wings were and imagined just how high he could fly. He tried to soak in some of Tiger's strength through his fingertips.

"What are you going to paint?" said Zavion.

"This is it," said Papa.

"No jazz band?"

"Nope."

"No fishing boat?"

"Nope. Just this green and then wait for it to dry and then another coat of green. Like a professional painter, right?" Papa looked happy. He was comfortable, way up there, balanced on a rung. He was comfortable anywhere if he had a paintbrush in his hand. "I spoke with your uncle Gabe yesterday. He says he has room for us."

"No!" said Zavion. Tiger squawked and flapped his wings. The *no* had more force than Zavion expected such a tiny word to have.

"Room for us for what?" he said quietly.

"To live with him."

"To live with him? I don't even want to visit him! Papa—" he said, trying to calm his voice as he scrambled inside his head for something to say. "It looks like you're painting another mountain on a wall."

"It's a green wall."

"Well, mountains are green."

"Enough with the broken-record mountain song over and over again, okay?"

Zavion watched Papa paint some more. He tried not to speak. He tried to keep the words from rising up like a wave and crashing over the levee. But sometimes waves have a pull and a push and a force that one single person can't hope to control.

"But it's true," Zavion blurted out. "They are green. Especially Vermont mountains."

"I've never seen a Vermont mountain, Zav. So I don't know if this looks like one or not."

"I doubt they're that awful minty color," piped up Ms. Cyn. She and Skeet came in from the kitchen.

"Morning," said Papa.

"I brought you some breakfast," she said, putting down a tray. "And I'll have you know that I made a personal visit to the kitchen to get it."

"Be impressed," said Skeet.

"I am," said Papa.

"I am too," said Skeet. "With both Ms. Cyn and you. Your painting job is excellent. Thanks for agreeing to repaint this room for me...." His voice trailed off. "You know what? I bet I could find you more painting work—for pay. Would you want that?"

Skeet was distracting Papa. Zavion had to keep him focused.

"Work is good," agreed Papa.

"I wonder...," Skeet mumbled. "I have an idea...." And then he was gone.

"You've seen a North Carolina mountain, right, Papa?" Zavion jumped in. "Isn't this the same color as Mama's mountain?" The paintbrush in Papa's hand shook the tiniest bit. "After Mama traveled to New Orleans and found you, didn't she take you back to North Carolina? To Grandmother Mountain? Didn't you get to see Mama's mountain?"

"Quiet, Zavion!"

The door slammed just as Papa yelled.

"Quiet!" squawked Tiger, directly into Zavion's ear.

Osprey ran through the room. Henry sauntered in behind her.

"Watch out for the wet paint," said Ms. Cyn.

"I told Gabe we would go to Kansas right away," said Papa, his voice quiet again. "There's no reason not to."

"You should come to Vermont first," said Henry. "That's a reason right there."

chapter 56

HENRY

Henry still wanted to take Zavion and Ben to Vermont.
He wanted to take Zavion up Mount Mansfield. He had told
Mom when she called.

"Why?" Mom had asked.

Henry was silent. He didn't know how to answer her. He
was surprised by his desire, actually. He had wondered if it
was a spur-of-the-moment thing, an idea he would feel was the
worst one he had baked up in his whole entire life, after he
had slept on it. But that hadn't happened. He didn't understand
why, but he felt even more sure about it than before.

"Well, I can't wait to see you—" Mom interrupted his
thoughts. "And I would love to meet your new friend." She
didn't ask again why he wanted to bring Zavion, which,
weirdly, made Henry miss her. "Brae's not the only one who
misses you," she said, as if she could read his mind.

"It's only been two days."

If he said he missed her too, he might cry.

"Well, I still can't wait to see you," said Mom. "With or without Zavion."

With Zavion.

Henry was determined.

At this moment, although he couldn't explain it or understand it and—Jeezum Crow, he would never say it to anyone else—he might tell Cora that taking Zavion to Vermont was his heart's desire.

chapter 57

ZAVION

"We don't know anyone in Vermont," said Papa.

"Of course you do," said Ms. Cyn. She tugged her scarf, which was about two miles long now, and gathered it into her lap as she sat down. "Who do you think you're looking at?"

"That's the problem. I don't exactly know."

"Him?" said Osprey. "He's Henry." She clicked to Tiger, who jumped onto her arm.

"No offense, Henry, but I've only just met you," said Papa.

"Henry," said Osprey, "I wish I still had that leash I gave you. I want to take Tiger for a walk."

"Tiger doesn't need a leash," said Henry. "I think he'd stay with you." He shoved his hands in his pockets. "I was thinking of taking a walk too," he said. "I need—I want to see Pierre's Salvation Army."

"Can't live with 'em, can't live without 'em," Tiger squawked.

Henry laughed, and Papa's face sharpened into anger. He

began painting again, and Zavion noticed his hand shook harder as he dipped the brush in the paint.

"That bird speaks the truth," said Ms. Cyn.

The door opened again and Jake walked inside. "Morning, everyone," he said. He stayed rooted just inside the door.

"Half the day is gone, lazy bones," said Tiger.

"You talk too much," said Jake, but he was smiling.

"Lazy bones! Lazy bones! Look what I've done today already—"

Zavion watched Papa. His face was still sharp. "Please, Papa—"

"Gabe is family," said Papa, but he wouldn't even look at Zavion when he spoke.

Gabe was family, but Zavion barely knew him. Where was he? Why wasn't he here?

Jake and Henry were here.

Zavion walked up a few rungs of the ladder and grabbed at Papa's ankles. "Please," he said again.

Jake cleared his throat. "I'm—uh—guessing this has something to do with a visit to Vermont?" He looked at Henry.

"Yup," said Henry.

"Henry talked with me about it. I'm happy to bring you and Zavion with us."

"Thank you, but no." Papa's voice was firm.

"You're welcome to come stay with Annie and me, Ben," said Jake.

"I'm not your damn charity case!" Papa slammed the paintbrush into the can of paint.

"I know you're not." Jake spoke quietly.

"No! No, you don't seem to know it at all! What do you think? That you can come down here with a few shirts and a few cans of soup and save us? Well, you can't! It's too little! It's too little and it's too late! Where were you before the damn levees broke? Where were you when they were cracked and needed to be fixed? A thousand cans of soup aren't going to build a wall high enough to keep that water out—"

Papa spun around and kicked the can of paint with his foot. It tipped and spilled. Green paint poured down on Zavion.

Zavion sputtered and gagged—

A flash—

Thick, cold—

"Oh, Zav—" Papa rushed down the ladder.

Oily, wet—

He closed his mouth. The paint tasted bitter.

Papa put his hands on his shoulders and guided him down the last few steps.

"Come on over here," said Ms. Cyn. She handed Papa something, and he wiped Zavion's face.

"Tighty-whities!" squealed Osprey.

"Papa—" said Zavion. The paint burned his eyes. "It isn't Jake's fault."

Paint dripped from the platform of the ladder to the ground. *Drip, drip, drip*, like rain.

"It isn't—" Papa's voice was quiet. He wiped his nose with the back of his hand. "But it's complicated."

"I don't understand."

"Can't live with 'em, can't live without 'em!" chimed in Tiger.

"Shhhhh—" whispered Henry. He sat on the floor with Osprey and Tiger on his lap.

Papa hugged Zavion to his chest.

"I don't know what to do," he said.

"I do," said Zavion through the paint that was still in his mouth. "We need to go to a mountain. I thought we needed to go to Mama's mountain, but now I think we need to go to theirs." He looked at Henry and Jake. "That's why I met them. That's why I went to New Orleans. That's why I found this—"

Zavion reached into his pocket and pulled out the marble—

HENRY

Henry gasped.

Wayne.

There was Wayne.

There was the mountain.

There was the marble.

The marble.

The flash of it between Henry's and Wayne's hands. The space lit up by the flash. The space between Henry and Wayne.

The flashing, pulsing, breathing space.

ZAVION

Zavion turned to Henry.

He knew instantly.

Here was the boy who had sent him the marble. In a million years Zavion wouldn't have guessed that he would meet that boy—Henry *here*. How far was Vermont? How many miles? Tree after tree after tree after tree, and all that highway, it was all compressed into this small space. The small, round space between one hand dropping a marble into another.

chapter 60

HENRY

"Do you want it?" said Zavion. He extended his hand to Henry.

Osprey leaned back into Henry's chest and looked up at him.

"It's a magic, isn't it?" she said. "It's *the* magic."

Zavion put the marble in Henry's hand. Henry let it roll back and forth on his palm. Tiger bowed his head and poked his beak at it. Henry couldn't believe it. He thought maybe he should feel excited to find it again, but a river of sadness rushed through him. An ocean. Wave after wave after wave.

"Where did you get this?" he asked. He wanted to be absolutely sure.

"I got some clothes from the Salvation Army," said Zavion. "The marble was in the pocket of a pair of blue jeans. These jeans, actually."

Henry scrutinized the jeans. A small rip at the knee. One cut belt loop. His old jeans.

"These ... are your ... jeans, aren't they?" said Zavion.

"Is there a hole in the right pocket?"

Zavion put his hand in the pocket. "A hole! Yes! The money must have fallen out—"

"Those are mine," said Henry, but he could tell that Zavion didn't need confirmation.

"Wow. So this is your marble?"

"Yup." Henry ran a finger from Tiger's head all the way to his tail. He missed Brae again. "Mine and Wayne's." He missed Wayne too.

"Who's Wayne?"

"My son," said Jake. Henry turned to look at Jake. He was staring at the marble.

"Henry's not—" began Zavion. Henry turned back to him. "You're not—"

"Henry's not my son," said Jake quietly. "Wayne is my son—was my son. . . ." He trailed off.

"We traded the marble back and forth. For good luck." Henry sighed. "I just—I wanted—but then I didn't think it had any luck in it anymore. So I stole it—I put it in my pocket—and then it ended up down here—" Henry uncurled his fingers and held the marble out to Zavion. "Here—"

"But this isn't mine," said Zavion. "Don't you want to keep it?"

"No—well, maybe—" Henry struggled. "I don't know—I don't think I will ever have any good luck again anyway—" All he had wanted was to find the marble, he thought he would feel better, and maybe even hopeful when he did, and now he was miserable.

Zavion extended his arm, but instead of taking the marble, he grasped Henry's hand like he was going to shake it. The marble sat between their palms.

chapter 61

ZAVION

"Ben?" said Jake.

"Yes?"

Zavion liked hearing that. *Yes.* The word *yes* coming out of Papa's mouth. He watched Papa wipe up some more of the spilled paint. Papa's face was turned toward the floor, but Zavion knew those eyes on the top of his head were looking right at Jake.

"You're a painter. A good one." Jake gestured to the freshly painted wall. "I'm not. Annie and I need our house painted. We're in need of a change." He paused. "And here's the other thing. I need to repay you."

"I don't understand." Papa looked up.

Jake spoke quietly. "You let me not be there. You might not even know it, and I don't even know if I can explain it. But for a little while, you let me be here. For that I will always be grateful."

Papa stood up. He walked over to Zavion, who silently handed him the marble.

"Let me let you not be *here*. Let me let you be *there* for a little while," said Jake.

Papa closed his hand around the marble. He climbed the ladder. He held the marble up to the wall, like it was the moon, or a planet. He was silent for a moment before he spoke.

"You think from way up there, high in the sky, the hurricane seemed so vicious? Seems like from that perspective it could have looked like a gray sky, a big wind or two, and a few heavy drops of rain, nothing much else." He took a deep breath. "Being right inside it, though—sweet Jesus—it made me believe in gods, or monsters. I keep seeing the walls of the house breaking apart around us"—he looked at Zavion—"me jumping and watching you jump behind me. I keep seeing you falling off the door. I keep feeling my hand slip, trying to find you in that water. Trying to get you onto the door." He tossed the marble into the air and caught it again. "Those roof shingles—" He opened his hand, the marble balanced in the center of his palm. "I can't seem to step any farther away than right smack in the middle of that damn hurricane." He turned to Jake. Even through his own sticky eyes, Zavion could see tears welling up in Papa's. "I owe you an apology for what I said before."

"No need," said Jake.

"Well, I am sorry," said Papa. "And maybe you're right."

Zavion opened his mouth but then promptly closed it again. The best he could do was be quiet.

But quiet was not Ms. Cyn's idea of best.

"Sounds like a good offer, Ben," she said as she knitted. "You need the work. I know you do."

"Jake's right too," said Henry. "About being a bad painter? Believe him. He isn't good at it." He turned to Jake. "Remember trying to help Wayne and me with that tree house? You painted more leaves onto the walls than were on the tree." He turned back to Papa. "Jake needs you. For the good of his house, you need to come."

Zavion held his breath. Papa was silent and still for a moment. Then he looked at Zavion and slowly nodded. "Okay," he said, tossing the marble to Jake. "Okay, we'll come."

Yes, thought Zavion.

JAKE

As Jake drove the truck up Highway 10, he thought about faith.

Faith.

At Jake's suggestion, Annie had contacted Margarita and was already learning Spanish. She told Jake that when she confessed to Margarita that she was afraid she might be too old to learn anything new, Margarita had said no one was too old to learn. She had said, *Faith is the bird that feels the light when the dawn is still dark.*

Only she had said it in Spanish.

La fe es el pájaro que siente la luz cuando el amanecer todavía está oscuro.

Fe.

Faith.

Fe.

Jake couldn't get the word out of his head.

It sounded like a musical note.

Sometimes a word could ring in the air like a bell.

Like a warning.

Like a celebration.

Like the marking of time.

The minutes ticked by as they drove up the highway. Henry sat by the window, his forehead pressed against the glass. Zavion sat next to Jake, asleep on his shoulder. Ben lay in the bed in the back of the cab.

The smell of cinnamon, peanut butter, and chocolate wafted through the cab of the truck, four slices of Cora's cake carefully wrapped for their journey. Jake couldn't believe their luck, not that he believed in luck.

Meeting all these people.

Making all these friends.

Henry finding the marble.

Maybe it wasn't luck.

Maybe it was faith.

A word like that reverberated. It didn't care if there was a fence or a wall or sixteen hundred miles of sadness between one pair of ears and another, it slipped inside any old way it could.

And so the word became a bridge.

A place to meet.

A place to connect.

Kind of like passing a marble back and forth, Jake thought.

He patted his shirt pocket, where the marble sat just outside his heart.

chapter 62
HENRY

Henry watched Jake hold the marble like it was the very world itself. Then Jake closed his hand around it and held it to his chest.

"I knew you took this from Wayne's casket."

"You did?"

"Yup. I can't explain why. But I just knew. Couldn't blame you."

"I'm—"

"Nah. Don't apologize. I mean it. No reason for one more thing to be buried in the ground."

"Jake, I don't know why I took it. I just—I wanted—"

Jake held up his hand. "No need, Henry." He held the marble against his heart for a moment and then opened up his hand. "You want it?"

Henry pulled his shoulders up to his ears and then dropped them.

He didn't know if he wanted the marble or not.

chapter 63

ZAVION

Zavion woke up in North Carolina and kept his eyes open all the way to New York. The highway up north looked almost the same as the Louisiana highway, especially at night. It stretched out in front of the truck for miles, gray and black and hard. But there were hills on either side of it, and in the faint dusky light, they looked like little countries to Zavion, one after the other rising up out of the earth, and the occasional tall tree looming high above the hills like a flag.

Zavion imagined he was trekking up and over each of the hills, leaving one country and entering another.

chapter 64

HENRY

It was cleaner along the edge of the highway here. Henry noticed that as he watched the yellow line whiz by. In Louisiana, there had been a steady stream of garbage. Here, he saw one lone black plastic bag, ripped, its insides spilling out along the shoulder of the road. And a dead raccoon. Henry wondered if the raccoon had broken open the bag.

The yellow line rushed by. Mile markers came and went. Each of the eighteen wheels of the truck turned like a marble. Over and over and over as Jake drove north.

Henry felt like an elastic band had been fully stretched, and it was now snapping him back home.

chapter 65

ZAVION

Right before they left, Ms. Cyn had given him a gift.

Zavion untied the string on the wrapping. A scarf. Zavion un-folded it. The scarf. He looked at all the pieces Ms. Cyn had added to it. One for each person he had come to know in this house. Tavius, Enzo, Skeet, and Osprey. There was even a piece of Cora's potholder, Pierre's cap, and the logo from Luna's grocery bag.

"I put something in there too," said Henry. "See the corner of my football shirt?"

"Almost had to tackle him to get it," said Ms. Cyn.

"And I almost had to tackle her back. You have enough of my stuff," said Henry. "My jeans, my marble—shoot, what else do you want?"

Henry was right. Zavion couldn't imagine wearing any other jeans.

"This one's mine," Ms. Cyn said. She pointed to a square of cloth that had a bird right in the center of it. It looked familiar.

"The banner!" Zavion suddenly remembered seeing it the first day he was here. The banner with the boy sitting under the tree and the book turning into a bird. The gratitude banner. It felt like a long time ago. "The banner is yours?"

Ms. Cyn nodded. "It's the only thing I brought from New Orleans," she said. "It's the only thing I was able to take from my house. Skeet made it for me."

Zavion looked up on the wall. The banner was there, but with a small square missing.

Zavion pulled the scarf tighter around his neck. It was colder up north.

chapter 66

HENRY

Henry had done one thing before leaving for Vermont.

Diana greeted them at the door. Parrots were in cages every-where—on tables, under tables, on chairs, on stairs, in hallways.

"Incredible, right?" Diana said.

"These are only a fraction of the birds that are missing." A man walked into the room with another woman.

"Lee is my son," said Diana. "And this is Dr. Burke. These are the boys I was telling you about. Zavion and Henry."

"I still can't believe you stowed away in our van," said Lee, patting Zavion on the shoulder. "Outstanding work." He shook Henry's hand. "And you—" he said. "Outstanding work too."

"Thank you," said Henry.

"You sure you don't want to stay and work with us?"

Henry hadn't been sure. Not at all.

"Lee is right, you know," said Dr. Burke. "In fact, these are only a fraction of a fraction of the pets that are missing."

Dogs flashed through Henry's mind.

Cats too.

One cat.

"I wish I could find them all," he said. He gripped the handle of Tiger's cage. "But what do I do with Tiger now?"

Henry opened the cage and sat at the kitchen table with Tiger on his shoulder and tried to answer all of Diana's questions. He tried to tell the whole story. He was pretty sure he hadn't left anything out. When he was finished, he listened to other parrots around him.

Words and bits of phrases.

Hello.

Who is it?

Come and get it!

It's about time.

Hello. Where were you? Hello.

Come back.

Hello. Hello. Hello.

When he was done listening to the parrots speak, Henry realized he had one more thing to add to their stories. "My friend—his cat—he had a cat," he said. "His name is Tiger too.

He's lost—the other Tiger. Please—find this Tiger's family. I think they're alive. And if they're not—I know a little girl who would love to take Tiger home."

While Henry slept in the truck, he dreamed of "This Little Light of Mine" sang by a chorus of birds.

chapter 67

ZAVION

Zavion must have fallen asleep again. As he stretched his arms over his head, he saw the edges of the hills in focus now. In the climbing light of the sun, he could see they were taller here.

"Are we almost there?" he whispered to Jake.

"Yup—" Henry's eyes weren't even open.

"Morning, boys," said Jake.

"Is it morning already?" Papa's gravelly voice came from behind Zavion.

The truck stopped at a T in the road. The sun rose up fast and a yellow glow seeped into the air. Jake put on his right blinker. "Henry's exactly right. We're almost there," he said. "Look." As they made the turn, a mountain appeared out of nowhere like the sky had birthed it just at that moment.

Zavion's heart pounded with excitement.

chapter 68
HENRY

Henry's heart pounded with fear.

chapter 69

ZAVION

"That's it, isn't it?" asked Zavion.

"Yup. Mount Mansfield," said Henry.

The mountain peak stretched across the golden horizon, long like Zavion's new scarf.

"It's such a long mountain range. I didn't expect that."

"The story goes," said Henry, "that it used to have a taller peak, more like a normal old mountain, straight up and down, and Native Americans would climb it to find a private place to wait when they knew they were about to die."

"You know the legend?" said Jake.

"You told it to me, Jake," said Henry.

Jake laughed. "Right."

"Like, a hundred times."

"Okay, okay—"

"So one day," said Henry, "a chief tried to make the journey to the top. He was hurt, though, and couldn't really climb, and he died before he reached the summit. God carved his profile into the mountain. That's why Mansfield looks like a face."

A face—

"Grandmother Mountain has a face carved into it too," Zavion said. He looked back at Papa. "We decided it did, anyway, didn't we?" Papa nodded.

"What is Grandmother Mountain?" asked Henry.

"I've heard of Grandfather Mountain," said Jake.

"They're near each other," said Papa. "Grandfather is part of the Blue Ridge Mountains, and Grandmother is across the valley. Pioneers thought they saw the face of an old man in one of the cliffs of Grandfather, and so they changed its Cherokee name, Tanawha, to Grandfather."

"My mama told the story that Grandmother Mountain was a wanderer," continued Zavion. "She never could settle, and moved from valley to valley, from river to stream, until she got lost one day, and she was scared. But in the morning, she saw a face come into focus as the sun came up, and she fell in love. It was Grandfather Mountain. And so she put down her roots and stayed forever.

"My mama was born near Grandmother Mountain," finished Zavion. "And when Papa painted the mural of it in my room, he painted the face of a woman in its highest cliff."

"An old grandma?" said Henry.

"No," said Zavion. "He painted my mama's face."

The truck was quiet after that. Zavion studied Mount Mansfield. It did look like the face of a man. The long face of a man staring up into the sky. Zavion traced the trail lines on the map from the base to the different summit points, traced the veins of the man's face. To the chin. To the nose. To the forehead. Up the winding line of one, then back down and up the line of another.

The truck mimicked his hand as it, too, wound up and down the dirt road, taking them into a new country.

chapter 70

HENRY

Henry made Jake drop him off at the bottom of the driveway, and Brae bounded toward him before he had gotten all the way up. Brae knocked him to the ground, his long body wiggling over Henry's.

"Hi, boy," said Henry. He buried his face in Brae's thick fur, breathed in the dog and dirt and pine that he had missed so much.

Mom was in the garden. She ran to Henry and gathered him into her arms.

"Oh, Henry—" she said. "I missed you—"

Henry collapsed onto Mom's shoulder. Brae ran in circles around them. Henry rested his chin on Mom's shoulder and squinted up at Mount Mansfield.

I'm back, he mouthed at the hulking mountain.

Mom squeezed him hard. "What an adventure you must have had. . . ." She trailed off. She pulled him upright and stared into his eyes. "Are you okay? What's wrong? Do you want to tell me about what happened?"

He did. He really did. But he couldn't remember any of it. Standing under the mountain, its long peaks golden with fall leaves, blindingly bright against the clear blue sky, its base brown and solid and never-ending, its rocks and dirt and the roots of its trees tumbling down and out, extending all the way to Mom's garden, made Henry's head feel empty. He looked down at his hand. Osprey's leash was wrapped around his wrist, like a reminder, like a string tied on a finger.

"Why don't you come help me weed?" Mom said. "Some Vermont dirt should make you feel better." She walked toward the garden. "And you can tell me about your trip when you're ready."

Brae took off, running in circles around the house, stopping to sniff a few trees and rocks, and then settled at Mom's side. He licked her bare feet, between her toes. Then he shot a glance at Henry and barked.

"Okay, I'm coming," said Henry.

Mom pulled a wilted flower out of the ground. "These poor marigolds," she said. "They look awful."

Henry knelt down. She was right. The whole garden was a mess. Weeds and grass sprouted up between the flowers everywhere.

"I've all but abandoned them this fall, haven't I?" said Mom.

She tucked her nightgown into her sweatpants. She yanked on a weed. Brae pawed at the ground, like he was urging Henry to help, so Henry yanked on the weeds too. "Oh, Henry—" Mom stopped weeding. "Watch this." She pulled a piece of paper towel out of her pocket. Then she pulled a marigold from the garden and wrapped it in the paper towel, like a present. She put it on the ground next to Brae.

No! No, no, no, no, no—

Mom squeezed one hand into a fist.

No! That wasn't how Henry did the trick!

Mom held her fist out toward Brae and slowly uncurled her fingers until her hand was flat.

Noooooooooooooooo!

Henry felt himself ignite.

Brae opened the present with his paws and nose. When he was finished, the marigold lay on the ground, not a leaf or a petal destroyed.

The flames in Henry's belly were so high they licked the back of his throat. They rose from his throat and up into his nose and eyes.

"Henry—" He heard Mom's voice through the roar inside him, but he couldn't stop it. He couldn't stop the heat and he couldn't stop the memory—

*　*　*

"Hey, you wanna see what I'm teaching Brae?" said Henry.

"Another trick?" said Wayne.

"Uh-huh."

"This dog could join the circus." Wayne sat up on his sleeping bag. "Okay, let's see it."

Henry tore a piece of cheese from the remaining chunk and grabbed a bandanna from the top pocket of his backpack. He wrapped the cheese inside the bandanna. Brae sniffed at it.

"You're teaching him to eat fabric? That can't be good for his guts."

"No." Henry shoved Wayne. "Watch, all right?" He stood up. "Sit," he said. Brae sat. "Good boy." He glanced at Wayne. "Good boy to you too."

"Shut up." Wayne swiped at Henry's leg.

"Okay, okay, I gotta concentrate," said Henry.

"Henry?" Mom's voice came back into focus.

Henry dug in the dirt with his fingers. He wanted to dig a hole so deep he could lay his burning body in it and smother the flames. He dug some more and hit a rock. Brae whimpered behind him. Henry had to get away.

He grabbed the rock and scrambled to his feet.

"Wayne!" he yelled, running toward the house.

Brae whimpered again.

chapter 71

ZAVION

It was time for Jake to go to bed. "We have a big hike to do later, right?" he said. "And the beginning of a painting project? Then I gotta get some sleep."

Jake began to leave, but then turned back to Zavion.

"This is yours, I think," he said.

He opened his hand. The marble sat in his palm. Zavion took it.

And with that, Jake disappeared into his room for a mid-morning nap. Annie led Zavion down the hall, past a closed door, to what looked like an office.

"I hope this will do," said Annie.

"Thank you," said Zavion. He stood in the middle of the room, taking it all in.

Annie opened the window just a crack. The cold air pushed its way into the room like a dog at the door.

"It smells—exactly like I thought Vermont would smell," said Zavion, breathing deeply. He coughed.

"Cold in your lungs, right?" said Annie. "There's nothing purer. Sweeps your body clean."

Zavion thought about the smell of bread baking. He already missed Ms. Cyn. He wrapped his scarf tighter around his neck.

"This is beautiful." Annie tucked in the end of the scarf. "It's good to meet you, Zavion. Real good," she said.

chapter 72

HENRY

"Stupid, stupid rock!"

Henry hurled the rock he had grabbed from the garden at the kitchen wall. A glass on the counter got caught in its path and crashed to the floor. Brae jumped at the sound and knocked into Henry's legs. Henry smashed his hip into the edge of the table.

"Stupid, stupid dog!"

Brae dropped his head and tail and slunk to the corner of the kitchen. He lay down. Henry felt a cold draft as Mom opened the door. Wind whipped the sky like cream. Henry glanced at Brae, who tucked his tail under his chin, trying to get his huge, lanky body as small as possible. Henry sank to the floor and put his head on his knees. He tried to breathe deeply, but the air vibrated in his chest and felt ragged like a broken fan.

He had let his best friend down. Henry took another broken breath. He thought he had left this in New Orleans, but he was never going to be able to let it go.

"Look at you two. You're both shaking," said Mom.

"I am not," said Henry.

"Well, Brae's shaking," said Mom. She got on her knees to pet him.

"No, he's not either," said Henry.

"He is." She buried her face in his neck and began to hum. And all of a sudden, Henry wanted her to come over and hum to him. Without lifting her head from Brae's fur, Mom said, "You want some hot chocolate?"

"Dogs are allergic to chocolate," Henry said. "Are you trying to kill him?" It just slipped out, the words all jagged from the blades of his broken fan breath.

Mom stood up and put her hands over her eyes. "I missed you so much, Henry," she said without looking at him. She clasped her hands in front of her face. "I wasn't talking to Brae, I was talking to you. You want some hot chocolate? And maybe some eggs?"

Outside, the wind continued to blow hard. It blew in small sideways bursts so it hit the windowpanes. *Bang, bang, bang. Bang, bang, bang.* Loud, little fists rapping on the glass. *Let me in, let me in, let me in.* Henry buried his head deeper into his knees. He didn't want to hear the wind.

"Henry—" Mom sat next to Henry. He felt her hand on the top of his head.

"I thought you were going to make eggs," he said to the floor.

"It isn't your fault."

He took a deep breath. "What isn't?"

"Look at me," she said. Henry lifted his head. Mom pushed on his chin so he was staring at her. "It isn't your fault Wayne died." She had tears in her eyes.

Henry tried to keep his head still, but his own eyes twitched and his neck felt like it was on a spring, ready to snap back from Mom. He swallowed back his tears. "Mom—" he said.

He was afraid to tell her. But he needed to.

"Yes?" she said.

"I was winning the race. I never won a race against Wayne. I ran past him. I ran way ahead of him." The words came out of Henry fast.

"Henry." Mom held the sides of his face with both of her hands, like she knew he was about to snap.

"I wasn't holding the marble—Wayne was—I messed up the balance—Wayne should have won—" Now Henry took a loud, gulping breath. "I shouldn't have run ahead of him."

"Oh, Henry." Mom brought her hands around Henry's cheeks, so that they were like blinders. Henry couldn't see anything except her face. She stared straight at him. "I don't know why Wayne died that day on the mountain. I don't. But I do know—with every bone in my body, Henry—that you didn't cause him to die. It didn't happen because you ran ahead. It didn't happen because of you at all. It isn't your fault."

He had wanted this, hadn't he? For Mom to come over and be with him like this? To say this? But Henry couldn't do it. He couldn't look her in the eyes for this long. He couldn't stay here. Stay still.

He snapped his head back and slipped out of Mom's hands. He scrambled to his feet. "I have to go," he mumbled. "I have to get out of here—"

"You can't keep running away—" Mom reached out to Henry as she got to her feet.

But Henry barreled out the kitchen door. Brae followed him. The wind pounded on his back as he ran. *You can't keep running away. You can't keep running away. You can't keep running away.* Henry still didn't want to hear the wind.

Or Mom.

chapter 73

ZAVION

Papa was on the phone when Zavion woke up. His voice got louder and softer and then louder again. He must have been pacing back and forth in the hall. It took Zavion a moment to remember where he was.

Vermont. Jake's house. Mount Mansfield.

And he had slept.

For the first time since the hurricane, he had really slept.

Zavion got out of bed. He opened the office door. Papa was making another trek down the hall.

"Skeet," he was saying, "damn, you work fast."

What was Papa talking about?

"No, are you kidding me? I'm there. Count me in."

"Papa," said Zavion.

"You said it! Hallelujah is right—" Papa kissed Zavion on the top of his head. "Morning, Zav," he said.

"What are you talking about?"

Papa put his hand over the phone. "Skeet says hi. He's running a business idea by me. A house painting company. A crew of artists helping to restore some houses at home." He practically hopped back down the hall. "Brilliant idea, Skeet. Oh, my bones are aching to be back in New Orleans."

Zavion tried to wrap his head around this new information. A job painting houses. In New Orleans. He walked into the kitchen. It was so warm and bright. He wanted to bake some bread. Maybe he would do that later. Annie sat at the table with a woman.

"*Soy una madre,*" said the woman.

"*Soy una madre,*" repeated Annie.

"*Bien!*" The woman put her hand on Annie's arm. "*I am a mother.* You said it just right."

Zavion walked outside just as Henry was running up the driveway. Henry sprinted to the house and slumped onto the porch, breathing hard.

In and out, up and down, went his breath.

Papa walked to the open window, the phone still in his hand. He yelled out, "Skeet says hi, Henry. Wants to know the name of an insect that can live for a few weeks with its head cut off. Nine letters." He paused. "He says you're the animal expert." And then he was gone again.

A dog bounded up to them.

"Wow!" said Zavion. "What is that?" The dog's nose reached for his hand. It felt cool and dry. The dog pushed his hand up and then kept walking so Zavion felt his head, his neck, and the length of his long body. Then he sat on Zavion's foot, his tail making a slapping noise against Zavion's jeans.

"Huh?" Henry seemed lost.

"Who is that?"

"Brae."

"Your dog?"

"Uh-huh."

Brae ran to chase a swallow that swooped low in front of them.

"Are you okay?" said Zavion.

Henry just shrugged his shoulders.

"I need to go up Mount Mansfield."

"I know." Henry seemed distracted.

"No, I need to go up now."

"Isn't Jake going to take you?"

"Please, Henry—" Zavion glanced back at the house. He knew he should wait for Jake, that it was the right thing to do, but he didn't feel like he could wait for one more minute.

Henry stood up. "I can't go," he said.

"But you said you would take me. You said you wanted to."

"I can't." Henry turned his back on Zavion. "Wayne died up there," he whispered.

Zavion put his hand in his jeans pocket when he heard those words. He grabbed the marble. He wasn't sure Henry had meant for him to hear what he'd said, so he was silent. He squeezed the marble tight.

He remembered Luna.

The sound of her bangles in his ear.

He remembered Mama.

You were you.

You are still you.

I love you all the same.

It was time for Zavion to make his own decision.

"I know you can't take me, but can you show me the way?" he said. "I have to go up that mountain *now*."

Henry was silent for a moment. Then he turned around. "I'll take you to the place where the trail splits," he said. "I'll show you the way to go from there."

chapter 74

HENRY

"Watch out!" a voice yelled.

A flash of silver barreled down the trail like a rabbit. Behind it, someone was running so fast that he couldn't stop himself. He tripped over Brae, who galloped up to greet him, and fell into Henry. Henry fell into Zavion. They all lay sprawled on the ground, stunned for a moment.

Henry spoke first. "Hey, Nopie." Brae nudged Henry with his nose and licked the ground under him.

"I dropped the can of tuna and then it was rolling down the trail." Nopie picked up the can and began to scoop tuna back into it.

"Oh, gross!" said Henry. Brae licked Henry's jacket. "Aw, you smell like fish, Brae! Get off me!" He struggled to stand up.

Nopie extended his hand to Zavion with a can still in it.

"He doesn't want that," said Henry, grunting as he got on his feet.

"I forgot I had it," said Nopie, setting it down. Brae's nose was in it in a flash. "Hi, I'm Nopie," he said.

"I'm Zavion."

"What are you doing up here?" said Henry.

"Looking for Tiger," said Nopie. "I thought he might come to me if I brought some tuna."

"And—"

"No sign of him yet. But I think he's up here. I talked to the rest of the neighbors on that one side of the road. Two of them saw Tiger. He was heading up the mountain. I'm sure of it."

The wind was getting fierce. Henry shivered and pulled the sleeves of his jacket down over his hands. "So why are you going back down the mountain?" he said.

"I ran up to the top. Left some tuna there. I'm working my way back down."

"You don't think some other animal—or, like, twelve of them—are going to eat that?" Nopie looked deflated. Henry felt bad. "You really think Tiger's looking for Wayne?"

"I know it." Nopie pulled his sweater up above his chin and breathed into it. "And I know he'll come back."

chapter 75

ZAVION

Zavion felt like he was in a different world, climbing up the mountain.

Everywhere Zavion turned, there was a plant he had never seen before. A tree he had never seen before. He thought about the few trees lining the streets back at home that had fallen. He remembered the oak tree that split just outside his house. He remembered his house. The church, the street sign, the swing set at the park. All of it blown over and cracked apart. He wondered if anything would be able to grow there now.

Here—where trees had fallen and were dead—was the bright green color of something new growing out from underneath.

chapter 76

HENRY

Henry stopped at the fork in the trail. This was as far as he would go. He pointed. "That way," he said. "That way will take you to the top."

"Henry—"

"Nah, I gotta go." Henry turned around. The wind was at his back now. It pushed him forward, it was so strong. Brae trotted in front of him. He sat and cocked his head to the side, confused. "What do you want to do, buddy?" said Henry. Part of him wanted Brae to come with him. Part of him, to his surprise, wanted Brae to stay with Zavion. He began to walk back down the trail.

"Henry," Zavion said again. "Please—"

Henry took another step forward. The wind rushed past his ears. He heard Mom's voice riding on it. *You can't keep running away.* He took another step away from Zavion. *You can't keep running away.*

You. Can't. Keep. Running. Away.

"I need you," said Zavion.

Henry turned around. Brae was sitting in the exact same spot, only sideways, one set of paws up trail and one set of paws down. Part of him ready to go up with Zavion, and part of him ready to go down with Henry. Zavion shifted from one foot to the other. He rubbed his hands together.

If Zavion could be brave, maybe he could be brave too.

Henry walked back to Zavion.

"Okay," he said. "Let's do it."

The sky was a medium gray, like the feathers of a Canada goose. But the wind was steady and strong, so the sky kept moving, sort of rippling, like a giant hand stroking the feathers. Nothing was staying still. Not the goose-gray sky, not the trees, not the grass and ferns that bordered the trail, nothing. Henry wasn't either. He just kept on moving. He was afraid if he stopped for even half a second, he wouldn't get himself going again.

"C'mon, Brae," he called. "We have to go up, boy!"

Brae raced ahead of him.

The sky was getting darker by the minute. Henry followed the white tip of Brae's tail like a flashlight. It was the only thing he could see. It was better that way, not seeing where he was going. Even though he could walk this trail in his sleep.

Brae began to trot, and then he ran and Henry ran with him.

"You with me, Zavion?" he yelled.

chapter 77

ZAVION

Henry ran ahead and Zavion panicked. A purple-gray color was inking its way across the sky. It was getting darker by the minute. And the air was thick, like soon Zavion's t-shirt, jacket, jeans, and sneakers would be covered in that same purple-gray color. He knew the color, and knew the feel of the air. It was going to rain.

Zavion thought he might smell that musty, windy, floody smell. He looked up.

"No. I am *not* in New Orleans."

He said the words out loud to keep that part of his brain— the part that might curl up into a ball and roll back to the hurricane, back to New Orleans, back home—to keep it straight and flat, to keep it connected to his eyes and nose and feet. He saw a tiny clearing in the bushes. He smelled a wet, piney, earthy smell. He felt the dirt and rock under his sneakers. He wrapped his scarf one more time around his neck. Put his hand in his pocket and felt the marble.

chapter 78

ZAVION AND HENRY

The purple-gray sky cracked open and the rain began to rocket down.

It was almost impossible to see. Zavion and Henry had to rely on their voices and hands to guide them.

"Are you with me?" Henry yelled. It was hard to yell into the wind.

"I'm with you," Zavion yelled back. It was hard to hear.

"Let's get off the trail," yelled Henry. "We'll be a little more protected."

"Okay," Zavion yelled back.

They stepped off the trail and walked into a denser, more wooded part of the mountain. The trees were close together here and their branches were like one umbrella overlapping another, and they slowed the crisscross of rain just enough for Zavion and Henry to open their eyes a little wider. Fallen logs lay across the ground, some perfect round tunnels and others caving in on themselves. Large groups of ferns fanned out like playing cards in someone's hand. And rock outcroppings appeared out of the ground every few hundred feet, small mountains amid the trees and ferns.

"Brae!"

The way Henry's mouth moved and his neck tensed made it clear that he yelled the name, but the word seemed to get swallowed by the thickness of the rain and the thickness of the trees, and so it sounded no bigger than a whisper.

"Brae!"

Zavion called to Brae, and his word was swallowed too.

But somehow Brae heard the boys calling his name and joined them off the trail.

The rain fell harder. Slivers thrown from the sky, the ground, the air around them, black and purple daggers, the color of a plum or a bruise. It got darker in the woods. The trees and ferns and rocks became shadows of themselves, and then they shape-shifted into other things. Scary things.

Henry saw Wayne. He saw Wayne at the start line as the sun was coming up, running down the mountain, lying at the bottom of the cliff, his bent leg, the blood, his wide eyes.

Zavion saw his Grandmother Mountain mural. He saw himself slipping on the door, slipping under the water, coming up once, flailing his arms, jerking his neck, sinking back down.

Henry and Zavion saw these things, but they kept walking. Their socks wet. Their necks wet. They kept walking until the trees became trees and the ferns became ferns and the rocks became rocks once again.

Zavion's toe caught on something and he fell to the ground. He tried to get up, but the leaves were slippery and he fell back down before he managed to scramble onto his feet. He ran to catch up with Henry.

Henry slipped on a wet rock and crashed into a tree. He opened his arms before he hit and thwacked the trunk with his chest. Hugging the tree, he turned to look for Zavion.

The sky lit up with lightning, and Zavion saw Henry waiting for him.

The sky lit up with lightning again, and Henry saw Zavion running toward him.

Henry wiped his eyes with the palms of his hands. "You okay?"

"Honest?"

"Honest."

"I have no idea. Are you?"

"I have no idea either." Henry turned to look behind him. "Now where's Brae?"

Zavion cupped his hands around his eyes so he could see a

little better through the rain. "I see him. He's over there. Under that ledge." He wiped his eyes with the palms of his hands. "Smart dog."

"Yeah, let's get under there too."

They ran.

Zavion felt, for a moment, like he was running a cross-country race.

Henry felt, for a moment, like he was racing Wayne.

They ran to where Brae lay huddled under a flat, protruding rock ledge. Henry unwrapped Osprey's leash from his wrist and clipped it to Brae's collar. "I don't want you to get lost, Brae. I know you're afraid."

"He's afraid?" said Zavion. He sank down onto the backs of his heels.

"He hates thunder and lightning. They terrify him." Henry buried his face into the wet fur behind Brae's ear. "Sorry I called you stupid," he whispered.

The boys peered out into the pouring, pounding rain.

Henry pushed his hand into the back of Brae's neck. "It's okay, buddy," he said.

"How do you know its okay?" said Zavion.

Henry stared at Zavion for a full minute. "I guess I know because of you," he said.

"Me?"

"Yeah. Check you out. Brae's not the only one terrified of this storm. You want to turn around?" Zavion shook his head. "I didn't think so. See? You're facing it. And if you can, well ... well ... so can I."

"But you already are. You're already facing it, climbing this mountain," Zavion said. "That's why I can."

"Nah, you are," said Henry.

"No," said Zavion.

"Yes," said Henry.

"No. No, you are," said Zavion.

"No."

"Yes."

The two boys threw their *Nos* and *Yeses* into the thick, dark air, and the words hit the rain like stones, making circles that grew bigger and bigger and bigger, cutting through the sheets of water. And in the spaces inside those circles, Henry saw himself tugging on Wayne's shoulder as he lay on the ground and Wayne opening his eyes. Zavion saw himself diving into the water and pulling up wood and shingles and glass.

The circles dissolved into the air one after another. *No* dissolved into *Yes* dissolved into *No* dissolved into *Yes*. *No*, Henry couldn't save Wayne. *No*, Zavion couldn't save his home.

But *Yes*—maybe *Yes*—they could help save each other.

From under the ledge, the boys stared out into the storm.

It was kind of awesome. The storm on the mountain—yeah, it was kind of awesome.

"Are you okay now?" said Henry.

"I think so." Zavion put his hand onto the back of Brae's neck. "He's not shaking anymore. I guess he's okay too."

And then—

The thunder and lightning stopped.

The rain and wind slowed down too.

They took a good look at themselves. Zavion and Henry were covered with mud. Brae was too. Three brown bodies breathing hard as the rain turned from daggers to drops, as the wind died to a breeze, and as the sky became up and the earth became down once again.

chapter 79

ZAVION AND HENRY

"What was that?" said Zavion.

He and Henry were back on the trail. The ground was muddy and full of puddles. They had to keep their heads down to watch where they stepped.

"Just a flash storm," said Henry.

Silent steam rose from the ground, like the earth was re-calibrating itself, letting go of some of the water that had just thundered down into it.

"That always happen up here?" said Zavion.

"No," said Henry. "Only sometimes."

Not that night, he thought.

The memory flooded back to Henry.

The bird on the wind swooped so low that the boys and Brae could almost feel its feathers. The last tree on the mountain, one of the red spruces just below them, rustled and they knew the bird had landed there, maybe settling in for the night.

Henry pointed at the bandanna. "Brae—" he said, moving his finger so he was pointing at Brae. Then he slowly moved his finger so it was pointing at the bandanna again. Brae grabbed the bandanna in his mouth.

"No, Brae," said Henry.

The tree rustled again. A lot. Too much movement for a bird to make. Brae got up off of the sleeping bag and trotted over to the tree, the bandanna still hanging from his mouth.

"Brae!" yelled Henry.

"You taught him to steal food?" said Wayne.

Brae bounded back to Henry and Wayne, his tail wagging, and then he doubled back to the tree. When he came back again, someone was with him.

"Awww jeeez," said Henry.

"Jeezum Crow," said Wayne. "Your timing is incredible."

"Did you actually follow us up here?" said Henry. Nopie was going to ruin the whole night.

"Nah, I come up here all the time—"

"Bull—" said Wayne.

"I do."

"You're full of it."

"It takes three hours and twelve minutes to climb the mountain from my driveway to this spot. I can turn off my headlamp in three places, I know the trail so well—"

"Okay, okay!" said Wayne.

"I love being up here at night," said Nopie.

"We love being up here at night," said Henry. This trail was his and Wayne's. This night was his and Wayne's.

Brae whimpered. He still had the bandanna in his mouth, so the sound came out muffled.

"You're teaching Brae that trick all wrong," said Nopie.

"Huh?" said Henry.

"That trick. You're trying to teach him to open a present, right?"

"Maybe—"

"The command has to be clear."

"It was clear—"

"Uh-uh. Just pointing at the bandanna is confusing—"

"What do you know about training a dog?" Henry's voice seemed to echo off the moon. "You don't even have a dog—"

"I trained my grandpa's corgi to count," said Nopie.

"A corgi's not a dog," said Henry. "A corgi's a pig that eats dog food."

Brae whimpered again.

"Hey, cool it, Henry," said Wayne. "Brae thinks you just insulted dogs everywhere—"

"Watch," said Nopie. "This is how you should teach him. Squeeze your hand into a fist—"

"Like this?" Henry stepped toward Nopie, both fists in front of his face.

"Whoa, chill, Henry," said Wayne.

"I'll show you." Nopie turned to Brae. "Drop it," he said.

Brae dropped the bandanna.

"Don't tell my dog what to do," said Henry.

"Good boy," said Nopie.

Brae wagged his tail.

"Shut up, Nopie!" yelled Henry. And then he pushed Nopie hard, and Nopie fell backward onto the ground. He jumped onto Nopie's chest and pinned him to the ground. He felt Wayne's hands under his armpits, pulling him up. He stumbled to his feet, elbowing Wayne back.

No one spoke after that. Nopie looked from Henry to Wayne, the whites of his eyes shining in the moonlight. He shook his head once, a small erasing gesture, Henry thought, and then tilted his head up toward the night sky. Nopie turned on his headlamp, a circle of light talking to the circle of the moon. He stood up.

"Nopie—" said Henry.

"Have a good night," Nopie said, rubbing the top of Brae's head.

Henry and Wayne watched him disappear into the darkness.

"You sure let him have it," said Wayne.

Henry looked down at his hands in disbelief.

"I don't know what happened," Henry whispered. He looked down at his hands. They didn't seem like they belonged to him. The moonlight made them seem larger than they were. Maybe they actually were larger. Like Wayne's size. He'd never pushed someone like that before.

"I can't believe you did that." Wayne wouldn't let it go.

Henry couldn't believe it either. Henry's face flushed with shame. He shoved his hands into his pockets.

Wayne pulled something out of his pocket. "Here," he said, "it seems like you could use this now."

"What is it?" said Henry. But he knew.

"The marble. Here, take it." Wayne held the marble out to Henry.

The marble felt ice cold in Henry's hand. "I don't want it anymore," he said.

"What do you mean, you don't want it anymore?"

"I'm done."

"But this is what we do. We pass it back and forth—"

"Didn't you hear me? I'm done. I'm done with this good-luck crap." Chills ran through Henry's body. Like the wind was blowing across his bones instead of across his skin.

Brae picked up the bandanna and dropped it in front of

Henry's feet. He sat, between Henry and Wayne, and looked from one to the other.

Wayne rubbed the circle on Brae's head. "Henry—so what if Nopie was right about the trick—it's okay, you know—maybe it's okay if he helps you teach Brae—" Brae stuck his nose into Wayne's palm.

"You have no idea what you're talking about!" Henry's chest felt hot. His eyes felt hot. "I'm done with this marble." He felt like a broken blender, buzzing inside, overheating, unable to stop. "If you don't want it, let's just throw it off the edge of the mountain."

"Jeezum Crow, Henry. This isn't the way we do it. We pass it back and forth for luck. I'm not going to give it back to you, you know," said Wayne. "Even if you want it, I'm not going to give it back."

"I don't want it. It doesn't work. It's crap." Henry shivered. "It's too cold up here to sleep. We need to go down the trail a bit." Henry picked up his sleeping bag.

"That wasn't the plan," said Wayne.

Henry walked close to Wayne. "We're changing the plan. We're changing a lot of things. Like this?" Henry held the marble up between them. "I don't need it." Standing there, eyes blazing in the night sky, Wayne did seem huge. "You don't need it either."

"You're wrong," said Wayne. He grabbed the marble and walked away, like he was going to walk right off the face of the mountain, but then he turned around and came back. He picked up the sleeping bag and stuffed it into his backpack. "You're dead wrong."

chapter 80

ZAVION AND HENRY

Henry told Zavion the whole story.

"We didn't talk much after that. And then we woke up and had the race and—" Henry squeezed his eyes shut. "I shouldn't have tried to win," Henry said, the words tumbling out. "I didn't have the marble. I wasn't supposed to win. It should have been like it always was. Wayne in front of me. Then I would have seen—then I could have stopped—" He scrambled up and stumbled over to the edge of the trail.

Zavion walked over to join Henry. Brae did too. The three of them stood at the edge of the cliff. The drop was steep, about fifteen feet to the ground. They stared over the rocky edge onto the top of a small tree, two jagged boulders, and dirt below.

Henry turned to face Zavion. "It was my fault. I said the marble was crap. I didn't take it. I should have taken it—that was the rule—"

Zavion stared at Henry. His face was soaked with rain, but fear was still visible underneath all that wet. Zavion saw it clearly on Henry's face. He knew that fear. All of a sudden he remembered what Ms. Cyn had said to him the evening he left Baton Rouge.

"You two are twins, you know."

Zavion laughed. "You're kidding, right? Henry's white and I'm black. He's short and I'm tall. He's wide and I'm skinny. He's from the North and I'm from the South."

He's from a mountain and I'm from a hurricane.

"He is sad . . . ," said Ms. Cyn, "And you . . . are sad. Do you see that, Zavion?"

Zavion squinted through the kitchen window. Henry was sitting on the grass tickling Osprey. Tiger flew up and down, landing on Henry's knee, then Osprey's shoulder.

"Henry has the same sad blue thing you have," said Ms. Cyn, "and the same scared gray thing." She turned Zavion to face her. "If you can feel it in yourself, you can feel it in him."

"Henry," Zavion said quietly, looking over the cliff, "it wasn't your fault."

The clouds were making a wider circle around the sun. Its rays filtered down through the trees and lit up the ground like it was singing its own sun-rendition of "This Little Light of Mine."

"You wanna hear something weird?" said Henry. Zavion nodded. "I felt more at home in New Orleans than I have felt anywhere else since Wayne died."

"I feel that way about this mountain." Zavion paused for a moment. "I sort of wish my mother had climbed it. I wish her face was carved across the pinnacle...."

The boys stood still. The woods seemed to stand still too. No rain falling. No wind blowing. Brae was on the ground between Henry and Zavion. He crossed one of his paws in front of the other and licked the mud from between his toes. His licking became the only sound.

Henry unclipped the leash. "Wanna climb to the top?" he said.

Zavion touched the marble in his pocket, tightened his scarf around his neck, and nodded.

chapter 81

ZAVION AND HENRY

They made it to the top.

The shiny white rock was jagged. It wasn't slippery like the gray rock had been.

"What is that?" asked Zavion.

"Quartz," said Henry.

A thick fog had rolled in and it was hard to see very far ahead, but the boys could place the heels of their shoes against raised pieces of quartz to keep their balance as they climbed up the last bit of the mountain.

A bird sang from a nearby shrub.

"What is that?" asked Zavion.

"A white-throated sparrow," said Henry. "They sound like chickadees underwater."

"You're kidding."

"They do, though, don't they?"

The bird sang again.

"Wow, yeah. They'd feel at home in New Orleans right about now."

They came around a bend and into a clearing. Instantly the trees became shrubs and the dirt gave way to long sheets of rock. The wind whipped through the air. Brae chased it, his ears perked up and his tail held high.

"What is that?" Zavion asked, pointing at the dense, low shrubs off to the side of the trail.

"Tundra," said Henry. "Cool, huh?"

"That's how high we are?"

"That's how high."

Henry wished they could see farther than a few feet in front of them. Zavion had come all this way and Henry wanted to show him the view.

Zavion walked closer to what he thought was the edge of the mountain, but then he stopped because he couldn't see far enough in front of his face and he was afraid of falling. He looked down at the ground instead.

"It looks like a marble," he said.

"What does?" asked Henry.

"The rock. Look at it."

The rock was swirls of gray and white and even green. It did. It looked like a giant marble.

Henry walked to the center of the largest sheet of rock. He

got down on his hands and knees and ran his fingers along its swirling lines.

How had he never noticed that before?

Brae stopped chasing the wind and stood still, his ears perked up high, and then he tore off into the tundra. Zavion took the marble out of his pocket and held it up to the sky. Its blue oceans and green mountains and its very own blazing sun broke through the fog and glowed.

Henry leaned over to look at the marble.

"Maybe this is Louisiana right here," he said, pointing to a spot of green.

"And this is North Carolina," said Zavion pointing too.

"So then maybe this is Grandmother Mountain," said Henry.

"And this is Vermont," said Zavion.

"And this is Mount Mansfield."

"And this is its peak."

"And this is—" Brae barked and Henry turned his head. "Jeezum Crow—"

"What?" said Zavion, turning to look where Henry was staring.

"Tiger," Henry whispered. Brae lay in the tundra, and walking back and forth under his chin was a small striped cat. Henry stared at Tiger, who finally saw him and stared back, his yellow eyes piercing Henry's. He sauntered over to Henry and Zavion. Henry dropped to his knees as if the whole sky had just pushed against his shoulders.

"Nopie was right," Henry whispered. "Tiger's been looking for Wayne."

chapter 82
ZAVION AND HENRY

The wind blew the fog away, and the boys could see down into the valley.

"I haven't seen color in so long," said Zavion.

"Yeah, New Orleans was gray," said Henry. "I mean literally gray."

Zavion laughed. "True," he said.

After they stood silent for a while, Zavion offered the marble to Henry. "Do you want this back?"

Henry took the marble in his hand. He stared at it. Then he pulled his arm back like he was getting ready to pitch a baseball.

"I could just throw it over the edge," he said. But then he dropped his arm. "Nah, I can't." He tossed it into the air and caught it again. Then he handed it back to Zavion. "I think you should have it," he said.

Zavion turned the marble over and over in his hand. "You're sure you want to give it to me?" he said.

Henry felt his boots standing firm on the rock. He felt the wind biting the edges of his ears. He peered into the valley, saw a break in the trees, and wondered if that was his dirt road, wondered if he could see his house. He glanced down. Brae and Tiger lay curled together on the tundra, their fur soaking up the sun.

"I'm sure," he said.

"Maybe Papa can help us paint a mural on that wall," said Zavion. "The one under the ledge. You know, where we waited out the storm? We could paint a face—"

"A few faces, maybe. That would be cool," said Henry. "Maybe we can ask Nopie to help." He shook his head. "I can't believe I just said that." He snapped his fingers. "Oh! Cock-roach!"

"Nopie?"

"Huh? Oh no, no. The answer is cockroach. The name of an insect that can live for a few weeks with its head cut off. Cockroach." Henry reached down to give Tiger a pat on the head. "Knowing Nopie, he probably can too." He and Zavion laughed. "Tell Skeet for me, okay?"

Zavion felt his sneakers standing firm on the rock. He felt the wind stinging the inside of his nose. He peered into the valley, saw a break in the trees, and wondered if that was the dirt road that led to Jake's house. He had done it. He had climbed to the top of the mountain.

"Maybe you can tell Skeet yourself. When you visit me in New Orleans . . . ," Zavion said.

"You think you're going back?"

"I think so," said Zavion. "I think Papa wants to stay there. I think I want to too."

"I'd like that," said Henry. "To visit you there."

"I could give you the marble when you come."

"I might want it by then."

"Until you come," said Zavion, unwinding the scarf from around his neck, "keep this, okay?"

ZAVION AND HENRY

It wasn't about luck. It never had been. The marble practi-cally had a string attached to it. Henry saw that clearly now. Zavion saw it. The marble had a sort of magic. Back and forth. Back and forth, weaving between them. And it wasn't just in the marble. It was in the whole world. The magic was in the space between. In all the pieces connecting.

In all the pieces connecting, falling apart, and connecting again.

The wind blew and the fog rolled right back in, covering everything. It was as if the valley had never been there. But it was there. Henry had seen it. Zavion had seen it. Like their joy and even like their fear, it would seem to come and go, but it didn't change the fact that the valley was there all the time.

The wind blew a third time, and the fog disappeared once again.

"Does that happen often up here?" said Zavion.

"Yup," said Henry. "All you have to do is wait a few seconds, and things change."

Henry and Zavion stood on the edge of the mountain, on the edge of the earth, where the sun and the moon shine over rivers and valleys, oceans and forests, cities and farmland. They breathed in and out, in and out, a spiral of mountain and river and air, a spiral of dog and cat and bird, a spiral of boy and boy and a marble traveling between them.

AUTHOR'S NOTE

Five years ago my life changed. Tropical Storm Irene swept through my state of Vermont, my town, my street, and *my home*—and all of a sudden I was inside *Another Kind of Hurricane* in a way I had never, *ever* imagined.

I know, now, how floodwater smells. How heavy flood mud is, and how it sticks to everything it touches. I know what it feels like to walk down a block lined with more refrigerators than trees and more garbage than grass. Facing cleanup is lonely—deep-in-the-bones lonely—and it's also a lesson in losing control. Part of that loss of control means surrendering to the awful thing that has happened, but another part means accepting help from friends and from strangers. And that's why I also know what it feels like to have a stranger walk up my front steps and ask if she can take the pile of muddy, wet laundry from my yard and wash it for me—and to not know what to say—and to finally say *yes*—and to have my life change forever because of that one word.

Put simply, that stranger and I—we became friends.

And this is just what happens between Henry and Zavion.

I got the idea for *Another Kind of Hurricane* from my oldest son, who, when he was four, asked the question, "Who exactly is going to get my blue jeans?" as we dropped off a bag of food and clothing for the Hurricane Katrina Relief Drive at the Vermont State Police barracks in September of 2005.

I read many articles and blogs and books as research for this story. I interviewed people. I watched countless documentaries. Hurricane Katrina was the largest and third-strongest hurricane to touch the United States, ever. It reached Category 5 proportions, with wind speeds up to 175 miles per hour and a storm surge—the rising of the sea based on atmospheric pressure and wind speed—of 20 feet high. About 80 percent of New Orleans was underwater during Katrina, and almost one million families in the Gulf Coast region were forced to live outside of their homes for at least a while. The list of incredible facts goes on and on.

But the facts don't describe the amazing people who were affected by Katrina. People like:

- Caleb and Thelma Emery, who, with their kids, took as many as twenty-five people at a time—mostly family, but not all—into their three-bedroom, two-bathroom home in Baton Rouge just after Katrina hit. Despite the chaos and loss, they were able to find joy and fun and a sense of community. These are the people after whom Skeet and his home are modeled.

- Donna Powell, who had only just begun her 911 Parrot Alert website when Katrina left thousands of birds homeless or trapped in homes. She immediately became the bird-rescue guru, traveling into New Orleans to search for birds and bring them back to her home in Baton Rouge, where she cared for them and tried to reunite them with their owners. Diana is based on Donna.

- Chris Cressionnie, a painter, who, after Katrina struck New Orleans, would drop his son off at school and drive his 1994 Chevy Blazer up and down the streets, looking for magnets on abandoned refrigerators, which he would then put on his car. My magnet artist is a tribute to Chris.

- Marco St. John, the artist turned house painter who inspired Skeet's business idea.

- And Ellen Montgomery, the woman whose practice of using roof tiles as canvases I borrowed.

That list goes on and on too.

After all of that research, I felt as though I knew—as best I could—what it had been like during those harrowing days of the hurricane. I felt emotionally connected to the incredible people who had survived such a tragic disaster. And it was from this place that I wrote *Another Kind of Hurricane*. I hope Henry and Zavion's story does justice to the resilient, beautiful people of New Orleans, but I recognize, after Tropical Storm Irene, that I can't ever know someone else's perspective exactly. What I've come to realize is that striving for knowledge and empathy, while accepting that we might not be able to totally get it, is truly the best we can do.

There is magic within the pages of *Another Kind of Hurricane*: how one boy in Vermont and another boy in New Orleans can come together in such a strange and stunning way. And I wonder, now, if my experience with Tropical Storm Irene is a part of that magic. Regardless, it has become an accidental author's gift—a window into the truth of my characters' lives. I am eternally grateful for that.

ACKNOWLEDGMENTS

A marble has magic when it is passed back and forth. This is the truth. And this book passed between the most amazing and generous hands, making extraordinary magic in the process.

My appreciation goes to Sarah Bertucci, Pat Bertucci, Leslie Helakoski, Alice Fothergill, Katie Speck, the volunteers at 911 Parrot Alert, Mark Waller, John McCusker, and Kenneth John Rayes, who kindly answered my questions about Hurricane Katrina. Thanks to Sarah DeBacher. Thanks to Laura Paul and the wonderful lowernine. org, and to Phil Bildner for leading me to them both.

Vital research materials informed this book, and I am grateful to their writers. Any logistical or factual errors are mine alone. Particularly significant were articles in the *Times-Picayune*, the book *Unfathomable City: A New Orleans Atlas* by Rebecca Solnit and Rebecca Snedeker, and the films *Trouble the Water*, produced and directed by Tia Lessin and Carl Deal, and *The Axe in the Attic*, produced and directed by Ed Pincus and Lucia Small. Chris Rose's *1 Dead in Attic: After Katrina* was invaluable. Many details in my book were adapted from his experience. I thank Chris for his generosity.

Thanks to the wonderful people at Vermont College of Fine Arts, especially Sharon Darrow, Julie Larios, David Gifaldi, and Margaret Bechard. To Uma Krishnaswami and Kathi Appelt: Henry and Zavion wouldn't have their story without you.

To the Unreliable Narrators, who are anything but unreliable, you rock. To Kelly Bennett, Trinity Peacock-Broyles, Erin Moulton, Kerry Castano, Katie Mather, Sarah Tomp, Cindy Faughnan, and

Sharry Phelan Wright: An *I couldn't have done this without you* that stretches from Vermont to Louisiana.

In 2008, SCBWI awarded me a runner-up Work-in-Progress grant for this book and PEN New England gave me a runner-up Discovery Award. Thanks to both incredible organizations for believing in my work.

A bucketful of gratitude to Jo Knowles, Adam Sherman, Lisa Condon, Kara Wires, Cody, Rebecca Roose, Hannah Rabin, Stef and Guthrie Hartsfield, and Alice Pollvogt. Thanks to Lee Rosen, Jean Kelly, Maryanne MacKenzie, Carole Coggio, Molly Dugan, Ellen Kraft, Amy Adams, Jen Heney, Sydney Long, Scott Kalter, and Dave Sobel. To Rae Barone, Ben Bush, and the On The Rise family: I could not have written this anywhere else.

I am deeply humbled by Jeannie Mobley, Liz Garton Scanlon, Audrey Vernick, Cynthia Levison, Jean Reidy, Laura Resau, Ruth McNally Barshaw, and C. G. Watson. You helped light this story's path. Thank you, Conrad Wesselhoeft, Mary Lyn Ray, and Mary Hershey too.

Erin Murphy, remember digging up that marble in your garden? You thought it was a good sign. Me too. How do I express just how much growing stories with you in the dirt means to me?

And, Annie Kelley, how did I get so lucky? Your grace, passion, and wisdom are as high and wide as Mount Mansfield. My respect and gratitude for you are the same. I adore collaborating with you. Thank you, too, to Anne Schwartz, Lee Wade, Rachael Cole, Colleen Fellingham, Christine Ma, and Christopher Silas Neal.

Huge hugs to my siblings and their children—Callie Smith; Dan and Jess Smith; Mia, Henry, and Cameron Smith; Rebekah Smith; Jordan Allard; and Tobin Calder—and to my parents, Hank and Kathy Smith.

Finally, unending love to Derek Miodownik and our children, Lucaiah, Zoran, Tavia, and Jafeth. The first draft of this story was called *A Marble Looks Like Home.* For me, home looks like you.

ABOUT THE AUTHOR

Tamara Ellis Smith earned her MFA in Writing for Children and Young Adults from Vermont College of Fine Arts. She lives in Richmond, Vermont, with her family. This is her first novel. Visit her on the Web at tamaraellissmith.com.